# RAIN CHASERS

**PART 1**
The Fairy in the Potting Shed

**PART 2**
Stargazers

by Lorna Uglow

Photographs by Charmaine Alexander
Designed by Cara Furman

*AuthorHouse™*
*1663 Liberty Drive*
*Bloomington, IN 47403*
*www.authorhouse.com*
*Phone: 1-800-839-8640*

*First published by AuthorHouse    05/03/2011*

*ISBN: 978-1-4567-7974-0 (sc)*

*Printed in the United States of America*

I hear the wind among the trees
Playing celestial symphonies;
I see the branches downward bent,
Like keys of some great instrument.

And over me unrolls on high
The splendid scenery of the sky,
Where through a sapphire sea the sun
Sails like a golden galleon.

Extract from a
Poem by Longfellow
*A Day Of Sunshine*

Dedicated to my grandchildren.
I hope the written word will inspire you.

# CONTENTS

## PART 1
## The Fairy in the Potting Shed

## PART 2
## Stargazers

# PART 1

## CHAPTER 1
# The Fairy in the Potting Shed

The noise was like a dozen butterflies beating their wings against a glass pane in a frantic effort to escape captivity. Enya was trapped in the potting shed, becoming increasingly frightened. The windows were covered in dust and spiders' webs that caught at her wings and dirtied her face. She fluttered upwards, her arms and legs lashing out in an attempt to free herself, but to her horror she was getting even more entangled.

The potting shed had stood for centuries, mostly unused, a haven for small rodents and insects. Ivy had grown across the door and around the windows, making it difficult to see inside. Enya, the youngest fairy in her clan or frolic of fairies, was sprightly and fun loving but often found herself in need of her siblings' protection. She had two sisters, Sorcha and Teagan, and one brother, Morgar, who was older and very handsome.

Unfortunately Enya's brother and sisters were not close when she had been trapped in the potting shed, so when she called and screamed there was nobody to help her. She grew tired and in need of a drink of nectar. Her wings could no longer flap so she lay for a moment suspended in cobweb, forlorn and dishevelled.

Outside the potting shed Olivia, who lived in the large house at the top of the garden, was thinking how she might make the potting shed into a den for herself and her cousin Maria, who was visiting from Devon. Olivia hated spiders' webs and was wondering if she should take the hosepipe into the shed and blast the windows when she saw something hanging from one of the webs. The thick ivy on the outside had grown in a circle, framing the window through which Olivia now gazed. In disbelief Olivia found herself looking into the eyes, not of a large trapped insect, but of a small exhausted fairy.

Olivia's first thought was that she must get to the fairy before a hideous spider could dart out and attack her, so prising the old broken door open, Olivia rushed inside towards the fairy who hung cocooned, afraid and dirty. At once Enya's wings began to flap in terror at the thought of being seen by a human. It was not widely understood amongst the fairies that if humans look into a circle of foliage it is possible to see through to where the fairies live. Only through a living portal of vegetation can they be seen and Enya now realised that the human was coming straight towards her.

Olivia, now afraid of nothing, loomed over Enya, delicately trying to untangle her before she could be damaged. "Oh, you poor thing, don't wriggle so - you're making it difficult for me to get you free. There now, I have you, but your wings are still full of cobweb."

Olivia suddenly realised, now that the panic was over, that she was actually speaking to a fairy. For a moment she found herself concerned as to what effect holding a fairy might have on her. Would she come up in a rash like she had done when she had once held a spiny caterpillar? Or would she start to sneeze as she did when she stroked a rabbit? She knew that her mother would be cross with her if she did touch something that she shouldn't. However, the concern that she felt soon vanished as she saw the distress that the fairy was in. The fairy's wings were bent and unable to open, caught up in strands of sticky web. The little fairy had tears in her eyes and all of a sudden she curled up in Olivia's hand, refusing to show her face.

There was a slight glow coming from the fairy, as Olivia tilted her hand this way and that in an attempt to get a better picture of the damage done to her.

"I want my bright light," cried the fairy. "I want my bright light."

"Your bright light," repeated Olivia, not able to guess what the fairy was asking for.

"Find my bright light," demanded the little fairy in a tone of voice that Olivia thought was verging on ill-humoured.

"I'll help you find your bright light if you explain what it is," replied Olivia, trying to console the fairy.

"My mama, she is my bright light!" shouted Enya, who seemed to become more anxious. The glow around the fairy shone more brightly each time she raised her voice and Olivia by now was losing her confidence, wondering what she had got herself into.

"Let me clean your wings first," said Olivia reasonably, but the fairy screwed herself into a tighter ball, wanting nothing but her bright light. Olivia thought she should take control of the situation, so looked around the potting shed for something to clean the fairy with. Not wanting to put her down lest she should get into more trouble, Olivia held the fairy gently as she rummaged for a cloth. There was a pot with old geraniums in it, however the flowers still had soft petals. Olivia plucked a petal and gently ran it over the fairy's wings, taking as much of the cobweb off as possible. Olivia was pleased that the fairy did not seem to object to this, so she continued to wipe at the tangle of web. The wings, Olivia noticed, were not as fine as a butterfly's wings and had pulsating veins running through them. They shone with the brilliance of rainbows; the colours, cascading and mixing, seeming to pour one into another almost like petrol on water. Between the wings on the fairy's fragile back was a covering of soft down the colour of wheat.

"There now," said Olivia with as much confidence as she could muster. "Your wings are almost clean, will you let me wipe your face?" The little fairy uncurled her slender body, slowly sat up, crossed her legs and held her face towards Olivia. At this point Olivia realised the enormity of what was happening. Her hand shook slightly making the fairy unsteady, but staring down into the most beautiful face Olivia had ever seen, she found it impossible not to shiver. She got goose bumps up and down her spine and into her hair and was left temporarily speechless. The beauty of the small fairy with huge green eyes, for some unknown reason, left Olivia with a lump in her throat.

"Wash Enya!" the fairy demanded, although now her voice was calm with no hint of bad temper. It was now Olivia whose emotions were in turmoil. Slowly she lifted the petal and dabbed at the fairy's face.

"Your name is Enya?" asked Olivia in an unsteady voice.

"Yes, Enya."

"I'm Olivia, I live in the big house at the top of the garden, would you like me to take you back to your mother - your bright light?" Olivia suddenly found the situation too much for her and wanted to return the fairy to the safety of her own world as soon as possible. For as much as it was wonderful to actually find a fairy, the truth of their existence and the fact that she knew of nobody else who had ever seen one, was almost too much for Olivia to cope with.

"Morgar will come for Enya. Enya must get clean and not have tears in her eyes or Morgar will be mad and boom something."

"Boom something", what does that mean?" asked Olivia, slightly concerned that she may be the target for this "boom."

"Morgar is to protect me, so when he thinks that I am in danger he throws his hand out like this, and boooom!" Enya threw out her own tiny hand, creating a shrill booom in the direction of the flowerpot that contained the geraniums. The pot instantly shattered, spilling earth and flowers onto the ground, causing Olivia to jump and Enya to laugh infectiously. Olivia too had to laugh at the spectacle and once she started she found she couldn't stop. Tears came to her eyes, and when Enya saw them she stopped laughing and a look of concern shadowed her pretty face.

"Olivia crying?" Enya asked.

"No I'm laughing, I've never seen a boom before." Enya looked puzzled which caused Olivia to start laughing again, but Olivia realised that the laugh was partly a nervous reaction to this wildly unbelievable situation that she was in.

4

"Who is Morgar?" Olivia's curiosity was getting the better of her now and she wanted to find out more about this fairy and the world in which she lived.

"Morgar is my rushing stream. My brother, he has the strength of a mighty waterfall and the speed of the strongest torrent. He protects me, and my two sisters Sorcha and Teagan."

"What of your father?" Olivia's interest was now all consuming as she heard about Enya's family.

"My father is my great oak. He is as steadfast as the oldest oak tree, with honesty and pride to match. He is always at my mother's side and she is his bright light too. You must have a family, Olivia?"

Olivia's imagination had been lost in this world of courageous and strong fairies and now, having been asked about her own family, she was slightly at a loss for words. For how could her father, who was an accountant, stand up to a mighty oak? Or her mother, who was a nurse, compare to a bright light? Thankfully Olivia had no time to answer the tiny fairy held delicately in her hand, for all of a sudden there was a mighty boom and another pot in the shed smashed.

"Come to Morgar, Enya." The male fairy that had arrived unnoticed seemed strong and formidable for one so small. He stood with legs apart demanding that Enya should go to him. Olivia was suddenly afraid, not knowing what magic these fairies were capable of - she certainly did not want to be on the wrong end of one of their booms. Enya tried to stand but the web still held her.

"Morgar, don't be cross, Olivia has been helping me."

"I don't want to hear, Enya. Your mother is not well, you must come at once."

In a trice Morgar flew over and whisked Enya away, snatching her out of Olivia's hand so quickly that Olivia neither saw nor felt the fairies' departure. Now, alone in the potting shed, Olivia could scarcely believe that she had not been simply daydreaming. The broken pots were now the only token that could possibly convince her that she really had seen fairies. She looked at her hands but there was no trace of web, dust or fairy. A chill went up her spine that told her that she should get out of the potting shed and into the safety of her house. Smiling to herself however, clinging to the memories of her secret, she entered through the kitchen door and saw her mother standing at the kitchen sink with Maria, her cousin. With a sense of mischief she crept up behind them, letting out a loud "boom" as she ran past.

"Olivia!" her mother chastised but Olivia ran on up the stairs to her bedroom to gaze out of the window in the hopes of seeing Enya again.

# CHAPTER 2
# The Rekindling
# Ceremony

Olivia's cousin Maria returned to Devon after a stay that was less than brilliant. Olivia did not tell her about her run in with Enya and Morgar, for she felt it was a secret that at this point should not be shared. She convinced herself that if she did share her secret with someone she would somehow put the fairy population at risk. She returned to the potting shed frequently but never caught another glimpse of the fairies.

Easter passed and summer came, a time that Olivia loved, as there was no school and she could spend long hot days in the garden. The greenhouse was a particular favourite of Olivia's as her father had collected many species of cacti and other unusual plants. She was watering the plants one day in her shorts and favourite tee shirt, deliberately dribbling water over her hands and legs, getting impossibly muddy feet, when she heard a familiar noise of wings against glass. Looking around, she saw Enya trying to attract her attention. The little fairy had not changed at all, even down to the rose petal skirt that she had been wearing when Olivia had last seen her. The top half of her body was entirely covered by the sheen of her long, blonde, wavy hair, her huge green eyes squinting with anxiety.

Olivia sensed that the little fairy was extremely distressed and remembered that Morgar, her brother, had said that their mother had been unwell when they had met in the potting shed. Rushing out of the green- house, Olivia nearly bumped into Enya who fluttered at the door. Enya hovered, a sense of urgency on her tiny face.

"What is it, Enya, is your mother still unwell?"

"It's worse than that, Olivia, the whole clan has become unwell. They are preparing the rekindling ceremony for my mother now."

"I don't understand, Enya, what is this ceremony?"

"Fairies don't die like humans, Olivia, their bright light fades when they are old or unwell and they need the ceremony to give them their bright light back. Each fairy has a bright light, we recognise each other this way. Infant fairies never get lost for they are always able to see their mother's bright light. Just like birds recognising the call of their young - they will only feed their own and similarly a fairy will only be attracted to his or her mother's bright light."

"I see, but how can I help you?"

"Olivia, there are too many of us unwell at the same time. We wondered if you might know what will cure us as it is something from your world that is causing the illness."

"Do you know what that might be?"

"We think it is the fumes from your cars. Our wings blister if we accidentally get too close to the smoke. Will you come to see my bright light, Olivia?"

"Of course I will but I'm not sure that I can help."

Olivia followed Enya to the bottom of the garden where a huge oak tree had grown for decades. The gnarled old trunk had sprung huge roots that protruded from the earth. They twisted and turned before burrowing their way back under the ground. At the base of the tree, lying on a large oak leaf, was Enya's mother. At a distance a frolic of maybe twelve fairies busied themselves with the preparation for the ceremony.

At a glance Olivia could see that Enya's mother looked frail and unwell. She reclined on the leaf, resting her head on a plump, fresh daisy. Her wings were spread out and Olivia instantly saw the damage that had been done to them. The glow of colours running through them was dim and there were blisters on them, some of the blisters having caused small holes to appear. Olivia felt a sense of shame to think that something from her world could be responsible for the cause of this disaster.

"Enya, what can I do? I have skin creams in the house, do you think that they might help?"

"We cannot use anything containing chemicals or man-made substances. Can you think of something else to soothe her wings before the ceremony?"

Olivia thought long and hard before remembering her father's greenhouse.

"I do know of something, Enya, come back to the greenhouse and bring a bowl."

Enya picked up an old acorn shell and flew after Olivia. In the greenhouse Olivia went straight to a green spiky plant that her father had been growing, called aloe vera.

"Enya, bring your acorn cup and hold it here." Olivia took a stick and pierced a hole in the side of one of the thick spiky leaves.

"My father says that the juice from this plant has healing powers. I'm sure this is going to help. Quickly, Enya, collect the juice in your cup."

Enough juice was collected and the two rushed back to Enya's mother. Enya gently dabbed the aloe vera juice onto the damaged wings and there was an instant improvement. Rhyannon, Enya's mother, smiled and looked up at Olivia for the first time.

"Stay child, you may come to the ceremony, they are nearly ready."

Olivia looked with uncertainty at Enya, for she was afraid of what might occur during the ceremony. What ritual would she observe, would it scare her? Too late to retreat, Olivia stood frozen to the spot, as the frolic approached. They carried what could only be described as a canoe- shaped stretcher that was carpeted with a bed of leaves. Rhyannon was instantly lifted onto the stretcher and the frolic hovered holding her up high, Enya's father at the head, a look of concern creasing his features.

Olivia watched mesmerised as Rhyannon started to chant.

"Speed little boat to the clouds in the west

They are rolling like waves; I am poised on a crest.

Wings take flight, be as quiet as a sigh,

Make haste for we chase my spirit in the sky.

Back to earth my wings will stay the fall
My frolic mourns; I'll hear their call
Not long, not long, I will return
And for you all my bright light burn.

The light that gave me life shines bright
I see her glow from this great height.
That light is me for I am she
We two apart will never be."

The lump in Olivia's throat was swelling uncontrollably until a tear rolled down her cheek. The stretcher was lowered and to Olivia's amazement it was empty. Nobody seemed concerned that Rhyannon had disappeared, in fact there seemed to be an atmosphere of celebration amongst the fairies.

"Enya, where has your mother gone?"

"To a place where our spirits go to replenish their strength and their faith. We believe that we will be reunited with our families and so we are. We must celebrate as we wait for her return."

The frolic made music, an eerie, haunting sound that seemed to whistle on the wind. It was gay but also emotional and Olivia had no idea how it was made. The frolic gathered, testing the aloe vera on their wings, smiling in a way that pleased Olivia, for she was determined to help them if it were at all possible.

The afternoon was becoming chilly and all of a sudden a strong gust of wind nearly swept the fairies off their feet. Morgar was furious.

"Bora – take care lest we harness you," he shouted.

"Who is Bora?" asked Olivia, who had been slightly scared by Morgar's sudden loud threat. Morgar came close to Olivia and once again, as she had done in the shed, she felt alarmed by his presence.

"Bora is the wind. He tries to catch us off guard and break our wings. His temper is increasing, for he too is suffering the effects of the fumes from your cars. His lungs are full of it and he tries to spit it out. Even the great oak tree has to bow before him as he passes. But don't be afraid of Bora, I will protect you, for you have helped our frolic. See how Brokk and Oberon have healed the holes in their wings with the juice from your plant. Brokk and Oberon, two male fairies, smiled up at Olivia as they spread their wings for her to see.

The colour rose in Olivia's cheeks for, although Morgar was small in stature, he seemed to Olivia to have a very brave heart and his gallantry flattered her immensely. Being observed by the three male fairies made her feel conspicuous and she was suddenly all too aware that her clothes were damp and dirty.

"You blush, Olivia." Morgar's chivalry turned to teasing, making Olivia uncomfortable, even more so when he let out a hearty laugh.

"Olivia, your face is beautiful. I have never seen such shiny dark hair and sparkling blue eyes. We do not judge you by what you wear. Fairies never change their clothes. When they are born their mother looks at them to see which flower their beauty should aspire to. Enya, for instance, reminded her mother of a rose, so she will always be adorned in rose petals. Ordella over there suits the white petals of a water lily and Sebille wears the petals of a lavender plant. What would your mother choose for you, Olivia? I think the long white and pink blossoms of a magnificent magnolia would suit your beauty!"

To her amazement Olivia looked down to see her slim body draped in the velvety petals of a fine magnolia flower. At the age of ten she had never been able to use the word elegant to describe herself, but standing before maybe a dozen fairies, smelling gloriously fragrant, she felt like the most beautiful princess. Her hair felt sleek and her body feminine, had she been given wings she would have taken to the air for the sheer joy of it.

The music continued and the fairies laughed and frolicked. They paired up and flew swirling into the air together, their wings beating against one another in what resembled play fighting. They would reach a certain height then rapidly descend back to earth, their arms swaying rhythmically with the music, only to rise fluttering into the air once more to repeat the manoeuvre.

"Enya, what are they doing?"

"They are enticing Rhyannon back to earth. Her mother pines for her, you see, Ordella waits for her return. Ordella will not eat or drink until her daughter returns."

"How long will that be, Enya?"

"That is not known. Rhyannon may feast with the spirits. She may seek guidance for her new life's journey now that she has been rekindled. It should not take too long. The clan will dance and be happy so that she will see what she is missing."

Food was laid out, nuts, pulses and sugar-coated rosehip doughnuts that were a delicacy, and so the fairies ate and drank and were indeed happy. Olivia tried to see where the music was made and eventually saw a structure of reeds held high for the wind, Bora, to pass through. Morgar came to Olivia to explain more about their ways and his concern for their future.

"We are afraid that the problem will worsen. Many frolics have left to find a safer environment. They mostly travel to the coast where the air seems cleaner, but we don't think that this is a permanent solution, for your aircraft fill the air with fumes too. Bora is becoming sick. We must find an answer."

Olivia was saddened by what Morgar had told her for she knew that there was a huge problem with air pollution. She had heard it on the news on the television and she knew that there would be no instant cure for it, but did the fairies have to suffer at the expense of humans?

Suddenly the chill in the air left and warm rays of sunshine broke through the dark clouds. The rays were so strong that they lit up the afternoon, shining down to earth, pointing to the base of the old oak tree. The atmosphere amongst the frolic changed and a sense of anticipation hung over the fairies. All eyes, including Olivia's, followed the path of sunlight. Looking up into the sky, Olivia had to squint and hold one hand above her eyes in an attempt to see through the light. The rays were dazzling but Olivia could see all the colours of a rainbow pouring down them from the sky to the base of the oak tree. She looked to the fairies for their reaction. Their expressions were serious, all playfulness gone, and their silence predicted a happening.

Ordella, Rhyannon's mother, came to the forefront and sat at the base of the tree in the direct light from the rays, her husband close by. She sat, hands clasped in her lap, staring up into the light, her lips moving as if speaking and yet she was silent. Time seemed to stand still. Olivia was becoming agitated when suddenly nothing more than a shadow could be seen at the top of the rays of light but the frolic burst into cheers and laughter. Ryhannon was coming home.

Enya fluttered around Olivia with the excitement and Morgar too looked relieved and happy. Rhyannon was sliding gracefully down a slow moving stream of bright colours that intermingled and sparkled. Her lilac dress seemed to blossom with life and her face was radiant. She slid down and knelt at her mother's feet and Ordella clasped her joyously. Enya joined them and the three created a light so bright that Olivia had to look away.

# CHAPTER 3
## The Court of Bardzak

"Olivia!"

Olivia jumped, a feeling of panic threatening to engulf her, as her mother had caught her in the midst of a frolic of fairies, wearing nothing but magnolia leaves.

"Come inside at once, supper is ready, you've been out here all afternoon and look at your clothes!"

Olivia's mother seemed to have the uncanny knack of creeping up on her just when she was least expected. How was Olivia going to explain her dress and the gathering of fairies, let alone the rainbow of light hitting the base of the oak tree? Olivia stuttered incoherently until her mother gave her a strange look.

"Olivia, why are you talking about fragrant petals? I think that is the last thing your muddy shorts remind me of. Now go upstairs and take a quick shower before supper."

Olivia looked down at her shorts then back to the base of the tree. Yet again there was no evidence that could possibly convince her, or anybody else, that she had not been simply daydreaming and that, of course, fairies did not exist.

With a sinking feeling Olivia took the stairs two at a time, threw her clothes on the bathroom floor and stepped into the shower. She had left the window open as she didn't like too much steam, but as she reached for the soap her eyes became blurred as a thick cloud of steam descended, threatening to choke her. Thinking this most unnatural, as the shower water was no more than tepid, she wiped her eyes with a flannel and was delighted to see the steam lifting as suddenly as it had fallen, leaving a message written on the glass shower door.

"The Court of Bardzak sits at midnight. Please attend. Enya"

Olivia's stomach churned with excitement at the thought of attending the court session. She had no idea what The Court of

Bardzak might be, but she was determined that she would be there. Her parents would be asleep by that time so she could creep out of the dining room window, which was at the back of the house, and straight into the garden.

Supper was a quick bowl of pasta followed by ice cream, a reserved conversation with her parents who were uninterestingly discussing financial matters, then back upstairs to plan what she would wear to The Court of Bardzak. Olivia said good night to her parents early then waited impatiently for the bewitching hour of midnight. She had dressed herself in her best jeans and jumper, tied her hair into a ponytail and wrapped a scarf around her neck, as the nights were chilly. She paced the bedroom floor quietly not wanting to be heard then, when she knew her parents were asleep, she crept down the stairs.

Peering out of the window into the dark eerie night Olivia began to wonder, for the first time since she had read her invitation, if she was not taking an unnecessary risk. She looked around the familiar room and appreciated the sense of security that her home gave her. She thought of her mother and father and knew what their reaction would be had they been aware of what she was about to do. However her curiosity got the better of her and she threw open the casement window, creating a door into the unknown.

She slid down from the windowsill and crouched for a moment to make sure that her parents had not heard her escape. All was quiet so she began to make her way down the garden to where she had left the fairies at the base of the old oak tree. Each twig that broke beneath her feet sounded like an explosion in the silence of the night. An owl flew overhead letting out an unnerving nocturnal noise, stopping Olivia in her tracks, giving her a second chance to change her mind and swiftly return to the safety of her home.

Too late - a fluttering movement at her right shoulder, like that of the largest moth, warned Olivia that she had been noticed. Morgar whispered in her ear that she was to follow him and his closeness once again unnerved her. Her choices had evaporated, she now felt obliged to follow. The glow coming from Morgar made the task easy although he did travel at some speed. He travelled at quite a distance ahead of Olivia but the light he was giving off was enough to illuminate the path down which she now hastened.

"Olivia," Morgar had made a sudden stop and had turned to face her.

"Olivia, we do not wish to frighten you but Bardzak has heard that you were able to help us with the juice from your plants. This is not written in our history. Humans have never before been capable of helping fairies and he wishes to sit with you. Will you do this for us?"

Olivia felt herself blushing again, held within the full gaze of Morgar.

"I will come with you, Morgar, but can you tell me who Bardzak is and what he may expect from me, for I'm sure I can be of very little help."

"Olivia, don't worry for you have already helped us greatly and if there is nothing more that you can do, then we are still in your debt. Bardzak or Bard Zak is a wise leader. He is a poet, bard means poet, and he has been rekindled more than any other fairy. He is a traveller and sits with each and every frolic, discussing their troubles and recording their successes. He has written our history in The Leaves of Gerfalcon, an ancient and precious manual that enlightens and instructs. He knows that we have reached a crossroads and that we must seek help or we may perish."

Olivia was in awe at the prospect of meeting Bardzak but agreed to attend this very important court session. Her heart pounded as she approached a clearing, with Morgar just ahead of her. She saw a spectacle that she found impossible to comprehend. A floating circle of a cloud-like substance hung in the clearing ahead of her, slowly rotating with maybe a dozen fairies sitting on top of it. At the centre a larger, more distinguished looking fairy acknowledged her arrival.

Bardzak stood; he was maybe a head taller than any of the

other fairies and dressed in a fabric resembling leather. He was handsome with shoulder length dark hair that stood out, as all the other fairies were blonde. As he addressed Olivia he remained facing her, as the cloud continued to rotate.

"Olivia, you are wise and have a brave heart. Will you join us on The Seat Of Gerfalcon?"

It has to be said that with the best will in the world, Olivia saw no way that she could possibly attempt to join the fairies on the floating carpet of cloud. She glanced to where Morgar hovered at her right shoulder and by raising her eyebrows and pulling a quizzical face made him understand her dilemma.

"Olivia, Bardzak wants you to join us on The Seat Of Gerfalcon. He intends to make you the same size as us. Are you ready to join us?"

Before Olivia could respond she found herself seated on the soft cloud gently going round and around. The sensation, however, was mystifying for instead of feeling that she was rotating, it seemed that the world was going round and that the cloud was stationary. She found herself seated next to Enya who smiled reassuringly at her, however Olivia's pulse raced with trepidation. Her legs were lost in the puffs of cloud but she felt a firm seat beneath her. She looked around the circle of fairies and found many eyes upon her. Olivia studied the fairies' faces, noticing how large their eyes were and how dense the covering of soft hair was on their backs between their wings. Morgar stood in the centre talking to Bardzak whilst Olivia tried to acclimatise herself. Enya touched her hand in a warm gesture and the two exchanged reassuring glances whilst studying each other's features at such close quarters for the first time. Olivia hadn't realised quite how fragile the fairies were, there seemed to be no weight behind them, Enya's hand was cold, her fingers slender as was her body.

"Olivia, you can return to your house at any time. We will not hold you here against your will."

"It's all right, Enya, I am comfortable now. I will stay to hear what Bardzak wants to say to me."

Olivia spoke with more confidence than she felt but she was determined to help if it were at all possible. Morgar seemed to speak for the frolic as he turned away from Bardzak and addressed his clan.

"We have all met Olivia and have acknowledged her help in the past. She has joined us now on The Seat Of Gerfalcon. Our quest is to cleanse Bora of the fumes that irritate him and cause his anger. Olivia may hold the key to solve this problem. Her people have the science to develop a cure."

Olivia listened in disbelief at this incredible statement. She had no knowledge of science and thought that magic must surely be the answer. Was it not possible for the fairies to throw out their hands to create magic as she had witnessed in the potting shed, or even better, to wave a wand? In truth she had not seen a single wand or indeed any magic except for the breaking of a pot or two, the inexplicable rekindling ceremony and the levitating cloud on which she was now seated resembling, for all intents and purposes, a wingless fairy herself.

Suddenly Bardzak took the floor, speaking directly to Olivia.

"Olivia, you have the bright eyes of an intelligent young being. We sense that you may be able to guide us in our quest. What would you say if we were to ask this of you?"

Bardzak spoke with an accent that to Olivia sounded Gaelic, she was not sure, for it was neither pure Scottish nor Irish but had a brogue all of its own. His beautiful dark blue eyes watched her intently as he stood perfectly still awaiting her answer, his thick brown hair blowing in the chilling night breeze, the mottled moon sending an icy glare.

Olivia had the urge to stand to answer Bardzak but Enya's tiny hand, held tightly in her own, kept Olivia seated.

"I have every intention of helping you in any way I can but I am only ten years old. I have not yet learnt any science; children would not be expected to achieve any sort of breakthrough whether that be scientific or in any other field until they are fully educated adults."

"Do your people not realise the exceptional bravery, imagination and enthusiasm of youth?"

Bardzak was visibly amazed at such a statement. He looked around the frolic interpreting their reaction.

"It is in the eyes of the young that we see our future. As fairies age they look backwards to their highs and lows, their achievements and their failures, they are recorded so that our children may learn from them. The young, however, look forward and it is in their eyes and their spirits that we find the path to our future."

Olivia had to agree that the older generation, in her opinion, were indeed staid in their ways but at her age she did not have the confidence of someone more mature, although she certainly thought of herself as brave to be sitting on a cloud holding court with a frolic of fairies.

Bardzak spoke again. "Tell me, Olivia, do you not sometimes have an original thought that sends your pulse racing at the prospect of achieving something great, something that no-one else has ever thought of; that thrilling notion of a great success or invention? It is that moment in time that you must grab and hold on to. You must not let it go or be forgotten, it is one such moment that can change the world."

Olivia's eyes were wide open as she listened to Bardzak and recognised something truthful in what he was saying. She had experienced such moments in time but of course, when shared with an adult, they had been dismissed. Her excitement grew, as did her confidence, as she recognised that she might indeed, with the help of the fairies, be able to achieve the impossible.

# CHAPTER 4
## The Wind of Change

Each fairy spoke in turn, giving Olivia the chance to get to know them individually. One smaller fairy called Meta, who had the prettiest face and thickest blond hair, spoke passionately about her fears and looked directly to Olivia for inspiration. Her plea was so overwhelming that Olivia flinched, consumed with guilt that her race had been the cause of the fairies' distress.

Suddenly Olivia was aware that each fairy had spoken, and the silence that had fallen over the cloud indicated that they were waiting for her to make a contribution to the court session.

So far, although each fairy had spoken at some length, no one had come up with any ideas on how to combat the problem of pollution. It seemed to Olivia that, although the fairies were intelligent beings, they lived in an innocent world that Olivia had very little insight into, and neither did they have any real sense of the world which she came from.

Having come this far, Olivia was determined that now in the spotlight she would not let herself look foolish. She remained silent for another moment, choosing her words carefully then stood apprehensively to speak, unsure if the cloud would take her weight.

"At this moment in time," she fidgeted, " I can give you little advice. I can go back to my world and learn as much as I can about pollution but there will be no instant cure. I can, however, tell you what little I do know. Gas does go into the air from cars and planes and also from the burning of fuels for our fires. The one fact that I can be sure of is that the leaves on trees take in that gas for their own use. The great oak may bow down to Bora, but he is sucking the poisonous gases out of the wind at the same time. Bora carries nourishment for trees but sadly there are not enough trees in the world to cleanse the air completely."

The fairies watched Olivia in silence. Their large trusting eyes were upon her, amazed at her statement; they looked at one another in bewilderment. Could the cure be so simple? Why did the fairies not know about the magic of leaves and why, if this were true, did the pollution continue to worsen? Finally Bardzak broke the silence.

"Olivia, is what you say true, is it indeed fact? Do leaves feed off the very gases that are poisoning us?"

"It is fact, Bardzak, but having said that, we humans have not as yet made use of that knowledge for we continue to chop down trees at an alarming rate even though this pollution is also affecting us."

"If this is so we must help each other. Never before have our worlds collided, it is a very dangerous time for us, Olivia, but with your help we may succeed in reversing the changes. But we have been serious long enough, life has become too worrisome - we must have some fun. I suggest a night of sport. You will join us for some games; we are in need of a champion to lift our hearts and our spirits."

The mood that had settled over the fairies, like the cloud itself, lifted at the mention of games. The fairies that had been so serious just moments before, now frolicked and jostled, laughing as if they had no worries at all in the world in which they lived. They seemed almost childlike in their instant mood change and Olivia realised how little she actually knew about them. Meta, the small fairy, flew to her and took Olivia's hand as if they were the best of friends. Enya joined them, taking Olivia's other hand and the fairies whisked Olivia through the air so quickly that she hardly noticed any movement, to a river not far from her house. Olivia knew it well, for she often went there with her mother to see the ducks, fish and occasional kingfisher, but never before had she experienced the river- bank from ground level nor arrived so swiftly by air. The night was dark and noisy, noises that Olivia had not heard before. She knelt amongst blades of grass that were as tall as she was, listening to nocturnal animals and insects whose voices were loud and to Olivia seemed slightly menacing. Her sense of smell was heightened, and the mud, water and surrounding foliage smelt damp, earthy and wonderful.

"What games are we about to play, Meta?" Olivia stayed close to Meta's side hoping for protection from she knew not what.

"We will surf the scented night breezes racing across the sky to greet the morning. The winner is the fairy to touch the first ray of sunshine as it emerges at dawn. We must beat the night, he will retreat in his defeat once morning has broken. The birds will hail the fairies victory with a dawn chorus and we will drink nectar from the lilies." Meta was excited at the prospect of this particular race, for she had once been the winner. She was indeed tiny but there was no doubting her courage or her agility.

Enya's preference was to mount a hawk moth whose curved hairy abdomen provided the perfect saddle on which to ride, his large wings, hanging forwards, provided strength and a means by which he could be guided. The river created an obstacle course over which both moths and fairies sped, maybe ten at a time, challenging the agility and stamina of their chosen moth. Fireflies illuminated a course, their flashing lights like cats' eyes on a road.

The men would do battle with one another by testing the strength of their wings, flying directly upwards towards the moon. The idea was to outmanoeuvre an opponent by disrupting his surrounding air currents, making his flight path less than smooth and leaving a clear path for the winner.

Others would balance on twigs trying to knock a friend or loved one into the water, whilst the younger ones simply flew in and out of trees giggling and having fun.

Olivia watched in awe of these fun-loving vibrant beings. There was no fighting or ill humour, they seemed to love and respect each other as humans sometimes tended not to. The games started and for a while Olivia sat alone, rather nervous because of her small size and lack of magic powers should she get into trouble of some sort, when suddenly she was startled by Morgar who came to sit beside her. The night occasionally fell into shadow as clouds slid beneath the moon but, having Morgar beside her, Olivia felt alive and happy, strong and important as she never had done in her own world. She studied Morgar with her dark blue eyes, her chestnut hair tickling her face as it blew in the wisps of wind. He was very handsome and, although the fairies' bodies were lightweight, muscles stood out through the fabric covering his arms and shoulders. His hair lay in abundance over his shoulders, joining the hair between his wings that was dense, almost like the hair on a bumblebee.

He didn't notice her watching him as he was laughing loudly at one of the fairies, Oberon, who had just had his feet dipped into the water by Brokk who had tipped him off a large overhanging twig.

Relaxing into the happy atmosphere, Olivia let her mind wander following a course of its own. The resemblance to insects the fairies showed gave her an idea that was so simple in its origin that she was almost too embarrassed to mention it. Why did the fairies not simply cross- pollinate plants or trees as insects do .The tallest could be crossed with the ones with the largest leaves so, if enough height and leaf expanse could be achieved, and with maybe a little magic, Bora might be cleansed. It would mean creating vast forests of a new species of tree- but who was to stop them?

Unsure of herself, she hesitated, waiting for the right moment to test out her theory. Morgar was engrossed in the games, anxious to take part himself. Suddenly he grabbed Olivia's hand and pulled her onto a huge hawk moth whose saddle was large enough for the two of them. The moth took flight before Olivia could protest and suddenly she was flying upstream with Morgar behind her. It was Morgar who guided the moth by skilfully pulling on one wing or the other. The speed thrilled Olivia who, once relaxed, found that she was so excited with the race that she felt like screaming. She laughed loudly, realising that they were in competition with several of the other fairies. Morgar and Olivia had the largest moth but, having to carry two on his back, he seemed to lose speed at one point and fall behind. Morgar was competitive and urged the moth forwards guiding him low over the water, in and out of tall lilies, until they took the lead flying swiftly upwards, making Olivia's stomach churn with the speed, motion and excitement. Oberon shook his fist playfully as Olivia and Morgar crossed an invisible finish line and slowed their moth down.

Olivia found herself flushed and quivery but managed to calm herself enough to study the moth. The hair on his body was dark and silky. He was graceful and silent; there was no noise from his breathing, even though he had exerted himself considerably during the race. He had black eyes and long antennae that reached out like feelers in Olivia's direction, as if he wanted to examine who had been riding him. A strange-looking fairy, colourfully dressed in the vivid orange-striped leaves of a tiger lily, came to the moth carrying a small pot which Morgar told Olivia was full of nectar. Her eyes were more slanted than the other fairies and were a deep shade of green. She held the pot up for the moth that extended a long coiled tongue and sipped delicately.

Olivia was intoxicated with the atmosphere of the night and never wanted it to end. However, she was beginning to think that she had been away from her home far too long and she was getting anxious to return.

"Morgar, I must get back home before my parents discover I am not there. There is something that I would like to say to Bardzak first. Can you show me where he might be?"

Morgar led Olivia back along the dank riverbank to where Bardzak sat, watching his frolic of fairies from the root of a gnarled old tree growing on the edge of the stream. His face looked sad and Olivia wondered if he was worrying about their future.

"Olivia, I hear that you have won a race. You must accept a

prize." He took from a pouch that he wore at his waist, a pod: long and green, it glistened in the shadows of the night. Holding out her hand she accepted the gift and asked what it contained.

"It contains ancient dust that has magical powers. It will not bring you wealth nor must it be misused, but when you are in need of it you will know what to do. You have wisdom."

Olivia wasn't sure if he meant that she was wise or that she held wisdom in her hand, contained inside the pod. However, she thanked him and simply explained her idea for cross-pollination.

He listened to her theory without an expression crossing his face then almost shouted, catching Olivia and Morgar's undivided attention.

"By the Eye of Koh-i-Noor!"

Bardzak stood in total amazement. His hand rubbed the faint stubble on his chin as he looked significantly towards Morgar who, anticipating his instruction, turned to Olivia.

"Olivia, let me take you home. Bardzak needs to think, the games are over."

Olivia was once again whisked through the air and found herself back in her own bed before she could speak. She had resumed her normal size and was, amazingly, in her pyjamas. Morgar had neither said goodnight nor could be seen anywhere, she wondered if she had said something wrong. She looked at her wall clock, the illuminated hands pointed to one minute past midnight, but how could that be, for she had not left her house until just before midnight? Had she really been with the fairies that night? Drowsily she closed her eyes, wondering if she was dreaming - until she felt the pod clasped tightly in her hand.

# CHAPTER 5
## The Coffer of Coeval

"Olivia, get up darling. We have to go shopping."

Olivia's mother had come into her bedroom with, in Olivia's opinion, the intent to annoy her. Olivia felt tired and irritable, not knowing why. She rolled over, keeping her eyes shut in an attempt to remain comfortably snuggled up and sleepy, but her mother had other ideas.

"It's a beautiful day, Olivia, let's get the shopping done and then go swimming."

Pulling the curtains open with far too much enthusiasm, Olivia's mother gave her a playful tickle on her back and then left the room. Trying to remain thought-free, attempting to go back to sleep, Olivia plumped her pillow, wriggled her hips trying to regain a comfortable position, then let out a deep sigh. Unfortunately the disturbance in her bedroom had had the desired effect and Olivia reluctantly opened her eyes.

Her bedroom was cool, a light breeze that tumbled through the open window billowed the curtains. Outside she could hear a mower coasting up and down on a far off lawn and her mother's voice laughing shrilly then gabbling to someone on the other end of the telephone.

"Olivia, breakfast is on the table."

Olivia wondered crossly how her breakfast could be ready when her mother was doing nothing but talk on the phone - as usual. Rolling on to her back and accepting the inevitable start to the day, she threw the bedclothes off and swung her legs out of bed. Steadying herself, with her arms stretched out behind her, she became suddenly aware of the pod still clasped tightly in her warm hand. The pod felt hard, a small stump at one end dug into her palm. She studied it carefully, wondering what it contained. Wisdom was what Bardzak had told her was inside, but what form did it take? Resembling a pea pod in shape and size, the only visible difference was the colour. Although one could vaguely say green, and in the night light when Bardzak had given it to her it had certainly looked green, it was a shade that Olivia had never seen before.

Have you ever tried to picture a colour that is not from this planet or tried to make up a new colour in your mind? Well, this had to be the product of someone's imagination. She did not have a word to describe it, for not only had she never seen the colour before, but also it was constantly changing. It was as if there was something living within, moving and regenerating, the colour becoming more vivid all the time. Well, as fascinating as it was, Olivia decided to hide it in her bedroom and get dressed. The problem with that was, every time she put it down and walked away, it returned to her hand. She put it in a drawer, turned to get dressed, and there it was back in her hand. She locked it in her jewellery box, put the key on a shelf, and there it was back in her hand. This was spooky!

Finally convincing herself that there was no way of tricking the pod into being left behind, she dressed quickly and went down to breakfast with the pod happily tucked away in the pocket of her shorts. By this time her toast was cold but she had no cause to complain for she had taken so long trying to persuade the pod to stay in her room. She ate her breakfast hurriedly as her mother was anxious to do the shopping before the day got too hot.

Olivia's mood had lifted by the time she jumped into the car and fastened her seat belt. However, the car seat was hot and sticky, the air muggy, causing her to fidget and frown, relentlessly peeling her clammy legs from the leather seat. She breathed a deep sigh of relief when they finally arrived at the shops. Olivia fiddled with the pod in her pocket the whole time that her mother was shopping. Her mother commented on her quietness and wondered if Olivia had a headache or was feeling unwell, but Olivia assured her that she was just hot and anxious to go home and get into the garden, unenthusiastic about swimming.

The shopping trolley was soon brimming with lots of appetizing things to eat, but Olivia found her mind on other things.

"Olivia!" A familiar voice shouted across the shop. It was Olivia's school friend who she hadn't seen for a while as she had been away on holiday.

Rosie and her brother Harry crossed the aisles of the supermarket to chat to Olivia. It was whilst chatting that Olivia got a sudden shock. She stopped in mid sentence for there, sitting on top of a large carton of extra thick double cream, was Meta.

The small fairy was beckoning to Olivia in a most persistent manner, whilst adjusting her floral skirt in an attempt to protect herself from the chill of the refrigerated section in which she sat. Olivia stuttered and completely forgot what she was talking to Rosie about, and searched anxiously for her mother. She saw her leisurely talking to Rosie's mother, seemingly in no haste to leave the supermarket. Fortunately it was obvious that neither Rosie nor her brother Harry could see Meta, for the fairy flew swiftly over and hovered in front of Olivia's face without any reaction from her friends at all. Olivia felt she would simply explode with the stress of the situation and frantically looked from the fairy back to her friends then back to Meta again.

"Olivia, are you all right, your face looks funny, should I call your mother, you've gone completely cross eyed?"

Olivia felt a sharp pain in her head, Meta was far too close for her vision to focus accurately and panic was causing her to become red and clammy.

"Oh could you, I have a really bad headache, I think it's the heat."

Both Rosie and Harry ran over to Olivia's mother to tell her that Olivia was unwell.

"Meta, what are you doing here, is there something wrong?"

"Olivia, they are going to form a night train, you must not be left out, for it was your suggestion in the first place. Morgar thinks it is not safe for you to come, but you simply must. We cannot go without you, Bardzak has said so, but Morgar objects"

"A night train", tell me quickly what you mean, Meta, my mother is coming."

Meta spoke so quickly and so close to Olivia's face that she couldn't understand a word the fairy said. In fact it caused Olivia to swish at her as if she was an annoying fly but Meta avoided her hand with great agility, taking no offence whatsoever.

"Olivia, what's the matter? I thought you were quiet. Sit down here while I pay for the shopping and then I will take you straight home."

Olivia continued swishing at the fairy, causing her to look extremely agitated until her mother became hot and flustered too.

Rosie's mother fussed over Olivia whilst Rosie and Harry argued over some sweets, seeming to make the situation even more heated. The shopping was paid for and packed quickly and Olivia was helped back to the car. Meta continued to hover around Olivia's head talking incoherently, but managing to cool the air somewhat with the flapping of her agitated wings. Then alone in the back of the car, out of earshot of her mother, Olivia calmed Meta down and listened to what she was trying to say.

"The night train, it leaves at midnight, you must be on it, Olivia."

In the blink of an eye Meta had gone. The pod seemed to be pulsating in Olivia's pocket, insisting on joining in on the excitement, whilst Olivia sat hot, confused and exhausted, trying to assemble the snippets of information that Meta had tried to give her.

Olivia's mother spoke persistently from the front of the car, worrying about Olivia's well-being, which only exaggerated Olivia's state of confusion.

"I'm fine, mum, just a little overheated and my legs are sticking to the seat again. I think I'll have a lie down when we get home."

Olivia did just that. As soon as she got home, she went straight up to her bedroom and flung herself on the bed to clear her mind and cool off.

"Olivia!"

Morgar's voice startled her, making her jump; her heart started to pound and her head did likewise.

"Morgar, what is happening? Meta says that you are taking a train, where is it going?"

"It is not a train as you know it, Olivia; well maybe if you think of a camel train crossing a desert you may get the picture. When a frolic needs to go on a long journey we travel in formation, one behind the other, connected by a force that you do not understand. We travel the night sky on a pre-planned trajectory. Bardzak will study the stars and plot our charts; he is guided by the Leaves of Gerfalcon. Have you ever seen a shooting star, Olivia? How many of those do you think were really stars and how many were night trains ferrying our travellers to distant places, our bright lights illuminating trails across the sky?"

"Oh, how exciting, I must come with you, Morgar, does it leave at midnight as Meta said?"

The pod fidgeted in Olivia's pocket expectantly.

"Olivia, we are travelling to Sarawak. We are searching for enormous leaves that have existed in far-off rain forests since dinosaurs roamed the earth. The journey will be hazardous, I do not want you to come."

Morgar stood on the bookcase looking down onto Olivia, his expression serious, and his mood sombre. Olivia's cheeks flushed with disappointment at the thought of being left behind, but then her temper took on a life of its own.

"I will not be left behind, this mission was my idea!"

Olivia stood; her eyes now level with Morgar's.

"I will come down to the oak tree at one minute to midnight and I will join your train. Please inform Bardzak of my intention."

The pod went quite still.

Morgar's eyes darkened, but he did not answer. Instead he vanished in a trice but not before throwing out his arm and sending off one of his most shrill booms that shattered a china ornament, one that Olivia had been particularly fond of. Kneeling on the floor she picked up the shards of china, holding the pieces gently in her hands, sad that she had caused Morgar to get so angry with her. She wondered if there would be a bad feeling between them when they met next and hoped desperately that they would still be friends. Obviously Morgar had regretted his action too, for as Olivia watched the pieces of her ornament held delicately in her hands, a warm feeling started in her shoulders, travelled down her arms and into the palms of her hands. The shards seemed to melt, and then reshape themselves until the ornament was as good as new. Looking up in bewilderment, she just caught a glimpse of Morgar before he vanished once more, a warm smile brightening his handsome face.

As promised, Olivia reached the base of the old oak tree at one minute to midnight. Her mother had checked on her constantly, making it difficult to prepare for her trip, but eventually the lights in the house had gone out and her parents had fallen asleep. Bardzak shouted across his frolic with a warm greeting for Olivia as she arrived.

"I was hoping you would join us, Olivia, although we were about to leave. The Leaves of Gerfalcon has revealed a diagram - a horoscope showing the position of the stars and planets and the exact moment that we must travel across a timeworn path on the outskirts of the universe. We must go prepared. We will meet many dangers but our search is a desperate one. Brokk, fetch the ancient Coffer of Coeval."

Brokk sped off to retrieve the coffer that Bardzak had asked for, leaving the frolic unusually quiet and serious. Both Enya and Meta stood by Olivia, glad of her arrival and respectful of her courage, for she had once again assumed the same size as the fairies. Morgar kept his distance although he did glance over to Olivia, giving a nod of his head in acceptance of her arrival. Olivia asked Enya what was kept in the coffer that Brokk had gone to get and the answer was surprising.

"Olivia, we know that humans think that we fairies carry

wands with magic powers. This is almost correct, although what we carry is not a magic wand. It is an ancient shaft made from a rare white metal called lanthanum that is contained within a sheath. It has been carved with symbols that relate to our origin. A bright light is held within; the same bright light that is inside us and around us at all times. The pure form of light inside the sheath does in fact have magic powers but they are difficult to harness, they have a free spirit like the great wind Bora, manifesting themselves at times of danger or despair. They can also be used as a beacon should we get lost or separated from our frolic. There are now only ten shafts left within our clan and they have not seen daylight for decades."

Olivia listened wide-eyed, the pod pulsating in her pocket, until Bardzak spoke again.

"My frolic, I have chosen the ten who must traverse the void on our path of destiny. Each must carry the Sheath of Coeval with a brave and hopeful heart. It is Olivia who has given us this hope, let her be the first to collect her sheath."

Olivia walked up to Bardzak to collect her sheath; her hopes that they would somehow manage to cleanse Bora of the sickening fumes were high, however her bravery faltered. It was only when Morgar came to stand at her side with eight more fairies behind them, each holding a sheath, that Olivia's spirits soared. Bardzak took the lead, chanting words that Olivia did not understand, a mist suddenly shrouded them, and then all Olivia felt was a weightless whooshing feeling as her legs left the ground.

# CHAPTER 6
## Night Train to Sarawak

The whooshing feeling soon subsided, to be replaced by the most tranquil motion that Olivia had ever experienced. She seemed to be enclosed – suspended - with nine fairies in a glass-like capsule, floating in complete silence through the most beautiful night sky. There was, in fact, no glass for she could reach out her hand and penetrate the capsule, the shimmering enclosure was simply a light force created by the power of the fairies' "bright lights" firing them across the universe.

"How do you like to travel at the speed of light, Olivia? Fairies have travelled this way since the beginning of time, before you humans were even aware of the concept of light speed. We are not as simple as you think we are. Isn't that right, Olivia?"

Morgan's teasing helped Olivia to take her mind off the enormity of her situation. She remained silent as she studied the stars, the huge globe with its mottled surface that was the moon and the revolving planet beneath her feet that was her home – earth. She studied the fairies again, now seeing them anew, fascinated by their capabilities and their complexities, wondering now if they saw her as a mere earthling.

One of the ten elite travelers was the strange-looking fairy with the slanted dark green eyes who had offered nectar to the hawk moth at the games. Dressed in the orange and brown stripes of a tiger lily, she seemed to glance at Olivia continuously until Olivia became uncomfortable. This fairy seemed to have strange mannerisms similar to those of an insect. Olivia watched her as she began to groom herself in the same way that a fly or bee would groom itself, rubbing her arms over the wheat-coloured down on her shoulders and over her head and face. She pulled down her wings and delicately smoothed them over, too. Olivia studied her in wonderment, the lack of gravity seeming to reduce movement to slow motion. Suddenly the fairy caught her watching and flounced her head away as if she was cross. Olivia felt herself blush, having been caught staring, and wondered if she had offended the fairy in some way. She had so far felt comfortable with all the fairies; it seemed unthinkable that she could make an enemy of one now.

Bardzak's chanting suddenly caught Olivia's attention.

"Oh qwerty Mugwump receive comme il faut

Our malmsey wine from the mandrake we grow.

No podsnap here - nor Kraken free

T'is the Elephant Ear we'll take buckshee."

The journey continued through time and space, the tranquility lulling Olivia into a complete sense of security. She was aware that she must be experiencing the same emotions that an astronaut would feel, however, the closeness of the fairies, in front and behind her, and the mystical qualities that they possessed, left her totally at ease and able to enjoy the wonders of the night sky.

The moments that passed seemed almost timeless; Olivia had no idea how long the journey would take, or had taken so far. Her mind seemed suspended in a space where time stood still but motion continued. She was neither hot nor cold, nor did she feel heavy or light, simply at complete ease. The fairies seemed calm and spoke amongst themselves quietly, as if in respect of the cylindrical travel machine in which they now crossed continents.

Bardzak's voice cut through the atmosphere.

"We have almost reached our destination, my frolic, have you all got a firm hold on your sheaths? We must stay together at all times in search of the enormous leaves called Elephant Ears. Olivia has indicated that we may be able to cross-pollinate them with huge trees in an effort to cleanse Bora. We will meet another clan who live in the vast rain forest that we are about to visit. I have sat with this clan before, they will make us welcome for we bring our malmsey wine to drink, however, we are not used to their land which is full of perils. We must watch each others' backs at all times."

At that moment Olivia saw out of the corner of her eye the strange looking fairy, whose name she now knew to be Nixie, staring at her again. The pod, clutched tightly in her hand, went cold as Olivia got the uncanny feeling that this fairy might do her mischief. She made an instant resolution to keep a sharp eye on her. This uneasy feeling that Olivia harboured was suddenly dispersed, however, as the bright light of the travel machine dimmed and their feet touched firm ground. They had travelled a night sky, so squinted as they stepped out into the bright sunshine of a rain forest that was only slightly shaded by the vast canopy of vegetation that stretched out, as would a large umbrella, on the wettest of days.

As Olivia's feet touched the ground the noise seemed deafening. Noises that were strange and frightening, for Olivia did not recognize them. The ground beneath her feet crackled and moved as if it had a life of its own and, to Olivia's dismay, she realized that the ground was indeed alive, for large beetles and weird-looking insects travelled beneath the carpet of damp leaves and twigs. In the trees above her head, birds squawked and monkeys dived from branch to branch with high-pitched screams and deep-voiced grunts. The look of fear on Olivia's face did not go unnoticed by Nixie who, to Olivia's dismay, was displaying a somewhat satisfied smirk. Olivia, in return, managed to achieve the most stoic of expressions and decided there and then that she would not let herself down again, for she wanted no one to think that she did not deserve her place on this adventure.

"Mugwump!"

Bardzak roared across the noise of the rain forest to a portly fairy dressed in a green robe.

"We have brought malmsey wine for you to taste, made from the choicest mandrake. Will you and your clan join us, for we have travelled far and we are in need of some refreshment?"

The mugwump or chieftain bellowed his retort.

"Bardzak, it is good to see you, please come - follow me, let us make you all welcome." The mugwump gestured that they should follow but not before giving Olivia a strange, almost intimidating backward glance. Olivia had set her resolve, however, and moved forward with as much confidence as she could possibly display.

The encampment seemed as well protected as was possible in this seemingly hostile environment, so Olivia took her seat willingly with the rest of Bardzak's clan. They joined the new and quite different frolic in a large circle under some huge bad-smelling fungi. Drinks were poured and handed out and soon the two frolics were at ease, drinking and merrymaking. Olivia drank the sweet wine with the rest of them whilst she studied this new clan. They were dressed quite differently from Bardzak's clan, the females adorned in the most spectacular iridescent feathers obviously collected from the forest floor. Their wings, too, seemed different, slightly more streamlined and certainly more colourful.

Olivia became aware of Morgar, Brokk and Oberon talking seriously to their rain forest companions until Nixie interrupted them and edged Morgar away from the group. At first he seemed disgruntled but Nixie smiled up at him in a flirtatious manner, at the same time casting a mischievous eye towards Olivia. Morgar too looked Olivia's way, leaving her wondering if Nixie was talking about her, but the moment passed as the mugwump addressed the party.

"Bardzak has explained your journey's purpose. My clan will help in any way possible. We have heard of a place where the great leaves blow in the breath of Bora; we will take you there now. We must cross the great rift that holds the body of Koh-i-Noor - the birthplace of rainbows. The journey will not be a long one, however the dangers will be many, especially for the one named Olivia."

Meta, who had kept her distance from Olivia on the journey, now came to her side as if to protect her. Meta was a small fairy in comparison to the others but Olivia sensed that she possessed great courage and was more than happy to find her to be a comrade. She smiled up into Meta's pretty face and the two seemed destined to become inseparable during the hazardous journey that was to follow.

The party of fairies set off on foot traversing the jungle-like terrain. They headed into the sun that glistened through fanned-out leaves and threw dancing shadows under their feet. The forest was humid; Olivia's heart pounded and beads of perspiration crept down her forehead, dripping unceremoniously on to her nose. Most of the fairies took to hovering over the bug-infested forest floor but Meta walked alongside Olivia. Nixie seemed glued to Morgar's side and for some unknown reason this annoyed Olivia intensely. As Olivia watched Nixie, she turned suddenly, catching Olivia's sullen look, and smiled with satisfaction as she spoke.

"Meta, could you come here a moment? I need to show you something that Morgar has found." Nixie's eyes seemed to slant even more than usual. Olivia was annoyed that she had not been invited to see whatever it was that Morgar clasped in his hand, but she did not want to show her dissatisfaction so she bent down to the ground in an attempt to make them believe that she too had found something of interest. Unfortunately she studied the barren patch of dirt for too long for, when she looked up, the party was nowhere to be seen. Worse still, her feet were suddenly whisked from under her as the forest floor erupted and she found herself on the back of a huge black millipede. It was like riding an unmanageable escalator or an undulating conveyor belt; she let out a scream as she fought to keep her balance. The pod spluttered out of her pocket, the stalk-like end flying open and with a cough, a puff of dust was expelled from the pod and a strange voice began to speak to Olivia.

"Do you think it wise to remain on the back of that creature?"

Olivia glared at the pod in disbelief as it hovered in front of her, she hoped that what Bardzak had told her about it was true and that it did indeed contain wisdom, for the creature on whose back she now jiggled was taking her off in the wrong direction and she felt incapable of making a rational decision on what to do next.

"I don't think it clever at all to be on this horrible creature, please help me."

"Do you not think it a good idea simply to - jump off?"

Olivia stared at the pod, wondering if his question was actually an instruction. Mulling it swiftly over in her mind she came to the conclusion that the instruction was in fact sound so she leapt unceremoniously from the millipede's back without injury.

"Very wise, Olivia, very wise."

The pod closed, leaving Olivia alone on the rough forest floor. However, at just about the time when Olivia thought she would burst into tears, Meta appeared in front of her, a worried expression marring her beauty. Meta hovered before Olivia and, for the first time since she had met the fairies, Olivia actually thought that Meta looked like the sort of fairy that you would find in a storybook. Meta was poised with the sun behind her, hovering gracefully with one foot behind the other, her wings outstretched, resembling a beautiful humming bird, and her sheath held high, as if preparing to grant Olivia a wish.

"Olivia, I'm so sorry I left you, it will not happen again, take my hand. Bardzak has reached the rift. You must witness the birth of a rainbow."

# CHAPTER 7
# The Land Where Rainbows
# are Born

Meta transported Olivia through the forest and into a huge clearing. The two frolics stood at the edge of a large crevasse, peering into its dazzling depths. The sun that had been so hot, now seemed less oppressive as clouds scudded across the sky throwing misshapen shadows across the savannah floor, evoking an eerie prediction of a mystical happening.

Olivia clasped Meta's hand tightly as they too squinted into the crevasse that sparkled with such ferocity that Olivia had to shield her eyes.

"What is in there, Meta?" asked Olivia.

"It is the body of Koh-i-Noor, the mountain of light, the stone that you call diamond. Your people have stolen the heart of Koh-i-Noor and hold it captive in a tower."

"Stolen it? How can that be; where do we keep it, Meta?"

"Your people aspire to wealth and Koh-i-Noor is very valuable. You only have a small portion of the diamond, the rest is in this rift and gives birth to rainbows. You hold her heart in The Tower of London, it has been there for many years, however it is rumoured that, if held by an imposter, it will bring nothing but misfortune."

"Then why do you not take it back, Meta? Surely by magic you could retrieve the heart that belongs here in this crevasse?"

"We cannot reach it, Olivia, for the Tower holds powers of its own. It is shrouded in dark magic that prevents us from being able to penetrate its walls. The magic comes from another era, a time long ago, and is too strong for us to compete with. We would lose many of our clan should we attempt to rescue it."

Olivia once again felt ashamed of the human race but, with little or no understanding of how humans had stolen the heart of Koh-i-Noor, she could on this occasion neither condemn nor defend her own people, so she became silent and watched and waited for she knew not what.

The two clans became restless. They moved in strange ways, ritually chanting, until they formed a perfect circle. Olivia found herself on the outside of the circle and completely excluded, being left with no choice but to sit and watch. She was relieved at being given the chance to rest, for the journey had been long and the experiences exhausting. The clans joined hands, walking, and then hovering, until at last they positioned themselves directly over the crevasse. At this point they began to flutter up into the air, occasionally beating their wings against each other in a similar fashion to the rekindling ceremony when they had been enticing Rhyannon back to earth. They flew low into the crevasse then shot quickly into the air with great agility, creating sparks of multicoloured lights. Olivia was mesmerized. All feeling of tiredness left her as she watched with total fascination.

The pace of their movements increased with the brilliance of the sunshine, for now all clouds had disappeared and the sky was a vibrant dark blue. As the sun reached directly overhead, the crevasse exploded with a magnificence of colour that Olivia had never before witnessed. Lights of all different shades shot out across the sky, forming a path into the unknown. A rainbow, thought Olivia, I have watched the birth of a rainbow.

The body of Koh-i-Noor sped across the sky with pure brilliance. Meta was later to explain that Koh-i-Noor went frequently in search of her heart. Each journey created a splendid path, a rainbow, down which she hoped her heart would return to her. The path formed an arch across the sky - it was as if her arm was reaching out, for she never gave up the hope of retrieving her heart.

"She goes with such splendour but always returns alone, it is so sad, so sad," mused the mugwump, who came to sit at Olivia's side.

"Olivia, look out across the savannah, do you see the large

fan-like leaves in the distance? They are the leaves for which you search. You must cross the plain in front of you, but be on your guard. There is an army of ants- giant ants that regard the land as their own. They will sense you coming and send out a patrol. They have tricks that will catch you out and a bite that can kill. We will go no further, for large numbers of fairies will be detected more easily. Bardzak must choose only five from your clan to accompany him; the rest will wait here with us. It will be up to Bardzak who he chooses."

Olivia was dismayed at the prospect of being left behind with the clan of the mugwump, so went immediately to Bardzak.

"Bardzak, will I be one of the five who go on to reach the giant leaves with you? I have come this far, please don't leave me behind now."

"Olivia, this is where it becomes dangerous. I do not think it wise for you to come any further. You do not have the knowledge or strength to use your sheath in times of danger. I think it best you stay."

Olivia's shoulders slumped with disappointment. Nixie smiled at Morgar, who seemed entirely unimpressed by her gloating.

"I will be on guard for Olivia. She will come to no harm."

Morgar came to stand beside Olivia and put his hand on her shoulder.

"Olivia has shown great courage, I will not leave her behind now. She will be there when we stand under the giant leaves and she will be the first to dance within the giant blooms of the Elephant Ears. This is my wish, Bardzak."

Nixie looked as if she would turn Olivia to stone there and then, causing the pod in Olivia's pocket to retreat as far as was possible and feel icy cold to touch, but Morgar stood his ground. He looked directly at Bardzak as if awaiting confirmation of his request.

"Morgar, you have the strength and courage of two, your wish is granted. Would each of you now choose one fairy to accompany us?"

Olivia waited for Morgar to make the first choice hoping with all her heart that it would not be Nixie, the pod in her pocket seemed to tense.

"I choose Brokk." Olivia breathed a sigh of relief and the pod relaxed.

"I choose Meta," said Olivia, causing Meta's face to light up as she came to stand at Olivia's side, a beaming smile slashing her face.

Bardzak then spoke the words that Olivia had feared.

"I will ask Nixie to join us. We, then, are the six who will cross the savannah. Our journey will not be easy but we go as one. Hold your sheaths up high; let them join for a moment as one bright light that we may see our path."

Olivia followed Morgar's lead and held her sheath up high. It was indeed heavy, causing her arm muscles to quiver but she would not be seen to falter. The six sheaths joined high over Olivia's head and a white light beamed out, pointing due west across the plain. Bardzak took the lead with Meta and Olivia following. Morgar and Brokk saluted the other fairies and the journey began, with Nixie trailing behind.

Brokk and Morgar took it in turns to scout the surrounding landscape, leaving no chance for ambush. Nixie looked churlish but Bardzak's attention softened her mood.

"Nixie, I have asked you to accompany us for you remind me of a beautiful butterfly who dances with flowers. When we reach the great leaves we must hope that they are flowering, for it will be your job to fly to the heart of the bloom to collect the pollen. This is the treasure that we must take home with us in an effort to cross- pollinate it with the seed of a large tree. At this very moment, Durin and Orin are gathering the seed from an American Coast Redwood, with this purpose in mind. If they too succeed in their task, then we may be able to achieve our dream and find a cure for Bora. We will create a tree so tall and with leaves so large that they will, in time, suck the poison from Bora's lungs."

Nixie was pleased that her part in this expedition was so important. Her mood seemed to change as her spirits lifted and each step she took became light and rhythmic.

The pod in Olivia's pocket, however, was not convinced by her sudden good humour and remained concealed and vigilant as the six companions continued their journey across the open savannah.

They encountered many strange life forms in the dense grass through which they passed: large lizards that barely noticed them and inquisitive insects that wanted to touch the travellers with their antennae. Olivia had to laugh when she saw Nixie use her sheath to give a good blow to the head of a large bug that was a little too friendly. None of these creatures, however, presented a threat and so the six made good progress.

The leaves were nearly within reach as dusk fell. Spirits were high as they quickened their pace, wanting to reach their goal before dark when the scent from the flowers would be at its most potent. A scattering of clouds scudded suddenly across the sky, eclipsing the moon and temporarily shrouding their path in darkness. When the moon shone once again, the travellers found that they had made a huge mistake. They had inadvertently stumbled into a massive web-like bivouac belonging to the army ants that were so feared. The nest hung suspended from a fallen trunk and the six travellers found themselves caught up in the middle of the structure. The bivouac was made up from the ants' bodies, clinging to one another by their jaws and their claws, protecting the queen and her brood from attack. To Olivia's dismay, she found herself suspended by her feet and arms in the midst of the nest. The bivouac was so dense that she had lost sight of her companions and that filled her with fear. Not only was she alone, suspended amongst an army of terrifying ants, but she had also dropped her sheath and could see it lying quite out of reach.

She was afraid to make any noise, for she thought it would bring attention to herself, and she was trying for all her might to blend in with the ants so as not to be attacked. The ants, however, seemed restless, causing the bivouac to swing precariously from the fallen trunk and the ants to pinch deeper into Olivia's flesh around her wrists and ankles.

"Olivia," said the pod. "Do you think it wise to dangle upside down for too long - will the blood not rush to your head?"

Olivia frowned, thinking the pod was making fun of her.

"I can't escape. I'm afraid that the ants will attack me once they realize that I am not one of them," Olivia whispered.

"Olivia, the ants are blind. All you have to do is smell like one of them and then you can move. Would it not be wise to rub your clothes against that large ugly ant to your right?"

Olivia found the courage to turn her head slowly and study the ant that gripped her so tightly; his legs were quite muscular, his large oval abdomen moist under a scattering of spiky hair. Realizing that this was where the scent was located, Olivia started to move slowly in his direction. His large blind eyes stared ahead, unfocussed but gleaming, whilst his antennae flicked this way and that in a state of constant alert. Olivia did her best to avoid the touch of an antenna, whilst pressing her clothing against the foul-smelling abdomen of the ant.

With a degree of success, Olivia caught the ant's scent on herself and her courage grew. She wriggled one of her wrists free from the ant's grip and began swinging her body in the direction of her sheath. It was no good, for the biting grip on her ankles had her shackled high in the bivouac.

"Would it not be wise to free your other hand, Olivia, before that vice-like grip draws blood? These ants are meat eaters, you know, and with the scent of your blood they may think a ready meal has arrived."

Olivia did not have to be told twice. The fear of becoming a ready meal forced her into action. Rubbing the scent from the ant over as much of her body as she could, she reached over and freed her other hand. The ant turned on her suddenly but when he caught her scent he relaxed. She freed one foot at a time, with no further reaction from the ant, and fell with a thud to the ground.

"Very wise, Olivia, very wise," mused the pod.

Studying the huge bivouac from the interior terrified her, for she could not see her companions within the oppressive denseness of the nest. The ants clung to each other, the huge net completely screening the outside. She could, however, reach her sheath and, once it was within her grasp, her courage returned.

Without thinking, she drew the ancient shaft from the sheath and swung it high into the air, she was about to wipe out the entire bivouac with one swish of the white metal when the pod shrieked.

"Would that be wise, Olivia, your friends are within the nest, do you think that they would benefit from your action?"

Olivia stopped just in time. The pod was right - she could have slain everyone with one slice of the shaft. What could she do, though?

"Would it not be wise to use the magic of the shaft?"

The pod spoke in a belittling tone that made Olivia feel quite inadequate.

"Pod, you must share your wisdom as never before, for I have no idea how to work the magic."

Olivia waited hopefully for an instruction but nothing came.

"Pod, please, our friends are in danger, they have all lost their sheaths, look, there are five sheaths under the log."

As Olivia looked at the five sheaths, she noticed a light glowing around them that seemed to brighten with each anxious word that she spoke. She suddenly knew in her minds' eye that the six sheaths must be joined as one. She ran to them and placed hers on top of the others, and the light created was blinding. She stood in the light, bathed in it, praying for guidance. Suddenly the pod spoke.

"Olivia, look down, you will notice that you are unable to see yourself, is that not so?"

"That's right, Pod. Am I blinded by the light?"

"Not blinded, Olivia. The bright light has shrouded you, making you invincible to the attack of formic acid that the ants will surely spit at you whilst you attempt to save your friends."

Olivia had to think quickly. The bivouac was restless and she could not interpret the mood.

"Pod, if I remove the queen, I think that the ants will follow, what do you think?"

The pod was silent but felt warm and reassuring, so Olivia wasted no time. Kneeling on the hard savannah floor, she saw a fault in the bivouac that led to the queen. She thought that she could crawl through it, so dropping onto her stomach, she edged forward, pushing with one leg. Although shrouded in light, the scent of the ants was still strong on her so, when she crawled through, the ants let her pass. Inside the heart of the bivouac, the stench was so great that it took Olivia's breath away. The queen reclined, attended by her workers, having many pupae and eggs scattered about her. Olivia's presence went undetected until she made a sudden grab for the queen. Holding onto her bloated abdomen, Olivia unceremoniously dragged the immobile queen across the rough ground, alerting a few of the closest ants that began to spit formic acid in every direction. The queen writhed as her fragile skin was grazed, but Olivia did not stop until both she and the queen were several metres outside the nest.

Sweat beaded Olivia's forehead as she watched the shape of the bivouac dramatically change, once the ants knew that their queen was missing. Like a stack of falling cards, the bivouac let go and fell into a mass of writhing bodies that in a wave-like movement thinned out and charged towards their queen. They swarmed over her, examining her, touching her with their antennae whilst the workers frantically collected her eggs and pupae, returning them to her side.

Out of this mayhem, five fairies rose from the debris that was once the bivouac. They retrieved their sheaths and came to kneel before Olivia, dirty faced and exhausted. Her quick thinking had probably saved their lives and they each saluted her, out of respect and a newly formed bond that each fairy now shared with her.

As she knelt amongst them, each resting after their ordeal, she squeezed the pod in her pocket, needing reassurance for the wisdom of her action. Her emotions were running wild as she studied the fairies but she found that even Nixie endowed her with a warm smile.

"Very wise," a voice resonated from her pocket, "Very wise!"

# CHAPTER 8
## The Gates of Dreams

As dawn painted the sky with orange and yellow lights, the fairies continued their journey. They had drunk plenty of nectar from the pottery jugs that were held at their waists and this seemed to sustain them. Meta had brought enough with her for two and shared her jug with Olivia, who relished the sweet nourishing drink. The Elephant Ears were now in sight and it seemed that nothing could stop them from achieving their goal. They passed a flock of greylags, large geese that were grazing on the moist savannah grasses and gabbling so loudly that the fairies could not hear each other speak. The sun was rising, warming the thick layers of the greylags' feathers, the day promising to be as hot as the last. Olivia looked across the even plain to the west, wondering what the disturbance was that caused dust to be lifted from the ground. As she studied the forming dust cloud, the flock of geese became suddenly silent and took to the air in unison, causing a massive down draught that nearly knocked the fairies to the ground.

"Morgar," Olivia caught his attention.

"What do you think that dust cloud is over there? It seems to be increasing in size."

Morgar shielded his eyes from the rising sun and studied the formation. Olivia had missed the aerial disturbance high in the sky that predicted a tornado.

"We must collect the pollen from the blooms as soon as we can for, if that tornado comes this way, both the pollen and plants will be destroyed. Bora is about to demonstrate his anger. Caurus, too, is in no mood for calm. If Caurus, the west-north-west wind, meets Bora head on, we will be in grave danger. Nixie," Morgar shouted, for the noise from the winds was increasing.

"Nixie, you must fly on ahead and begin your job as fast as you can. There will be no time for rituals or dancing, for it seems that both Bora and Caurus are headed this way intent on a collision."

A spiralling column of air was forming within the clouds; a vortex that could wipe out the frolic in an instant, for they could not defend themselves against Bora when he chose to display his strength and anger.

Nixie looked scared, reluctant to go on alone. Meta, giving Olivia a reassuring glance, volunteered to go with Nixie but Morgar refused the request.

"Nixie, you must fly as fast as you can. Collect the pollen and then seek shelter. We will try to distract Bora and Caurus and head them off in a southerly direction. Now fly, fly like the wind."

Nixie did not falter or question the command but, as she turned to fly away from the group, a strange expression crossed her face and she made a sudden grab for Olivia's hand.

"Olivia should come with me, she will not be able to endure the force of the tornado. I will take good care of her, Morgar."

Morgar was distracted by the imminent danger, so did not argue with Nixie. He seemed to give it only a second's thought, and then gave his approval with the nod of his head. As Olivia watched him, a feeling of apprehension churning in her stomach, he gave neither a word of farewell nor a backwards glance. Olivia was left totally reliant on Nixie; a nagging sense of foreboding was now to be Olivia's constant companion.

Olivia's wrist was clasped tightly in Nixie's hand as they flew through the air that was becoming saturated by the dust storm. Olivia dropped her head in an attempt to breathe clean air but the wind was throwing the dust upwards into their faces, causing the two of them to choke and their eyes to sting. Nixie seemed to have strength enough for the two of them and fought courageously against the tempest, flying swiftly upwards until the air cleared and the sun's bright light shone once again. Looking down they could see the swirls of dust-laden air crossing the savannah floor, engulfing every living beast that had not been fast enough to flee. They saw, too, the frolic making their way to the forefront of the spiralling tornado that now reached down like an almighty arm from the sky to the ground. Nixie shouted over the roar from Bora,

"We must fly east away from our frolic, Olivia, don't be afraid."

Olivia, to her own amazement, suddenly felt confident in Nixie's ability to keep them out of danger and was slightly ashamed of having had bad thoughts about her in the past. Olivia grasped Nixie's wrist with her free hand and squeezed it in a gesture of trust and friendship as the two flew with great speed towards the Elephant Ears. They had now completely lost sight of the frolic and could only wish them luck in distracting both Bora and Caurus long enough for them to collect the pollen.

Nixie descended rapidly, their landing jolting them, causing the two of them to run forward a few steps before coming to a stumbling standstill. They were at the base of the most enormous stems that Olivia could ever have imagined and she gazed up in awe. To her disappointment, she could not see a single bloom, only tree-like stems opening out into dark green leaves so large that they could have eclipsed a tennis court. A tremor of fear ran up Olivia's spine as she heard a roar from Bora, bellowing in the distance. She thought of the brave frolic sailing close to the wind on a wing and a prayer, and hoped against all odds for their safe reunion.

"Olivia, we must concentrate on the task at hand. Do not take your mind off our mission, for we must not fail. Our time is limited; we must search for the blooms and collect the pollen. If the frolic fails to distract Bora, he could be upon us at any moment."

Once again, Nixie took Olivia's hand and flew her into the air. They climbed high, using gentler air currents to lift them above the Elephant Ears, enabling them to see if any of the plants were in bloom. On top of the canopy, they found themselves bathed in an intoxicating fragrance that, coupled with the rhythmic wafting of the leaves, was almost hypnotic. It enticed them to rest, to dally in a state of relaxation that Olivia would certainly have succumbed to, had Nixie not jolted her back to reality.

"Olivia, look, there is just one bloom and it is full of pollen. We must collect it quickly and then seek shelter, for Bora is groaning in defiance, he does not heed the frolic and he is getting closer."

They landed on the most beautiful flower. It was white and as soft as satin, narrow at the base and fanning out at the top. Yellow fluffy stripes lined the interior and from far down inside rose five stalk-like pollen-bearing stamens. They were laden with pollen, more than enough to fill the pots that they had brought with them for the collection. The scent was overpowering, pouring into the air with the sole intention of seducing insects into the bloom. Olivia felt a little dizzy, as they made ready to relieve the stamens of their precious bounty, so she held tightly onto Nixie, who lowered her into the bloom. Once inside, Olivia was protected from the elements. The wind's force was increasing and with each moment the flower bent and swayed with more vigour. Nixie was hovering at the entrance to the bloom, making ready to tap the pollen into her pot, when she was startled by the arrival of the largest beetle imaginable. The huge male rhinoceros beetle had climbed unnoticed up the outside of the flower and now rose, tank-like, over the outer lip of the bloom. Its large horn-like mouthpiece preceded the body, resembling a cannon then suddenly, as his balance shifted, the beetle tipped forward and fell heavily into the bloom.

Olivia screamed as the beetle lunged forward towards her, his armoured legs with hooked, serrated claws grazing her skin as he passed. She lashed out at the head of the beetle, causing him to make a loud hissing noise and an attempt to retaliate. He tried to turn but his body was too large to manoeuvre within the restraints of the bloom so, much to Olivia's relief, he descended to the pit of the bloom, his weight accelerating his progress.

"Olivia, please do not dally, Bora is approaching, and we have only minutes." Nixie now had to shout to be heard over the noise from the winds but Olivia got the message and the two of them forgot the beetle and collected the pollen into their pots.

The job done, Nixie grabbed Olivia's hand and the two shot off into the darkening sky. Bora was by now treacherous and seemed to follow their every move. There was no sign of the frolic and Nixie's concerns for their safety were mounting. She swerved to the left and Bora followed, to the right and he was close behind. Caurus too was on their tail; did they not want a cure for their polluted breath?

Nixie flew tirelessly on but Olivia's strength was fading. The mounting noise was deafening, making it impossible for the two to communicate and their breathing became laboured. Nixie could feel the life draining out of Olivia and knew that she must make a rash decision. She drew Olivia right up next to her, their cheeks touching, as she tried to outrun the winds.

"Olivia, you must trust me. We have no hope of outrunning Bora for much longer. I need to trick him, please listen carefully. I am flying towards The Gates Of Dreams, Bora cannot pass through them. When we get there we must make sure that we go through the gate made of horn. This will ensure that our dreams will come true. If we are blown off course and go through the gate made from ivory our dreams will be barren. Do you understand?"

Olivia had barely the strength to answer but the importance of their next few moments was obvious, as Bora was already making their flight unsustainable. Nixie's struggle to keep control over their direction was becoming impossible and her strength too was fading. Grit stung their eyes, causing tears to flow freely down their cheeks. Suddenly Nixie hugged Olivia even closer to her and whispered in her ear.

"Olivia, your dream, what is the dream you wish to come true?"

"My dream is for us to succeed, to stop the pollution, and yours, Nixie, what is your dream?"

"I wish to share my bright light, Olivia. My dream is for

Morgar to see my bright light only – as my eyes see none but his."

Tears stung Olivia's eyes, as she suddenly understood Nixie's strange behaviour towards her. Nixie had been jealous of Morgar's attention to her. How ridiculous for she was a human, Morgar a fairy. It seemed so simple - but love of course is blind.

"Nixie, our dreams will come true, yours and mine. You will have Morgar and we will cleanse Bora. Quickly, let us pass through the gate."

Nixie smiled, a warm smile that confirmed that at last they trusted each other and she made one last valiant effort to reach the gates before they were overcome by Bora. Alas, the winds were upon them. They clung to each other with a valour that becomes heroes but Bora ripped them apart.

Olivia was toppled through the air without protection or direction, cascading forward, thinking that there would be no tomorrow. Strangely though, her fears evaporated as she was thrown in timeless wonder and her body relaxed. A light brought her thoughts rushing back and she caught the outline of some magnificent gates up ahead. The light was Nixie, she saw her out of the corner of her eye. Olivia shouted...

"Nixie, which gate did you say to take? Ivory or horn?"

"You must go through the gate made of horn, Olivia."

Time seemed to change its pace and the world slowed down. Olivia saw the ornate gate made from horn with its twisted carvings and mosaic symbols. She manoeuvred her body, as would a skydiver, so as to guide herself through it. The elation that she felt, however, at having succeeded, plummeted as she saw Nixie fail to cheat Bora and was blown struggling through the gate made from ivory.

"No, no, no," she shouted at the top of her voice. "You will have Morgar." The separation from Nixie was too much to bear as she spiralled headlong into oblivion.

"Olivia, darling, you're dreaming."

Her father sat on the side of her bed stroking her hair.

"There now, that's better, you've been shouting in your sleep.

You're sweating, darling, would you like a drink of water?"

Olivia felt the grit in her eyes and the scratches from the rhinoceros beetle stinging her legs. Her hair was dishevelled and her body ached.

"Here, let me tuck you in, you've thrown the bedclothes off. Tomorrow you can tell me all about those wonderful plants of yours growing in the greenhouse. I've never seen anything like them before, they put my specimens to shame."

Olivia leaped from her bed to gaze out of the window at the greenhouse. The moon was full, like a mottled pearl in the night sky, illuminating the garden and a greenhouse full of thriving saplings. She saw Morgar standing alone at the base of the oak tree surveying the crop that was to secure a future for everyone, but there was no Nixie.

"Come back to bed, Olivia, the plants will still be there tomorrow. What do you think, that you will wake up in the morning and find it was all just a dream?" he laughed.

"No, father," she replied with a dry hoarse voice, " not a dream, they are what dreams are made of, you'll see."

Hither, like you ancient Tower,
Watching o'er the River's bed,
Fling the shadow of thy power,
Else we sleep amongst the dead.

Wordsworth
Hymn (Jesu! bless).

# PART 2
## Stargazers

# CHAPTER 1
# Bright Lights

"And here is Lara with the weather."

"Thank you Sophie. A bright start to the day over most of Britain, and once again I am pleased to report that the air quality continues to improve. The rest of the week looks settled, a good time for getting into the garden, but make the most of this spell of fair weather as, towards the end of the week and into the week-end, a band of rain will be coming in from the west, across the northern parts of Ireland and into Scotland. The south will remain dry and bright but with a cold westerly breeze. Now, I'll pass you back to Sophie for a news update."

"Thank you Lara. Scientists remain optimistic regarding the sudden diminishing levels of air pollution, giving way to clear blue skies over most of the world this morning. However, now that the sun seems brighter and the rain cleaner, scientists are baffled by the absence of rainbows. Speculation is intensifying amongst the world's top meteorologists that damage done to the ozone layer may have something to do with the loss of our much loved rainbow. Now, in other parts of the world:-

Swathes of an enormous tree covering vast areas of the Amazon Basin and India are taking some of the credit for the improvement in air quality that we are experiencing. The new species of tree, as yet unclassified but aptly nick- named "Colossus," has sprung up from the devastation caused by logging companies in the regions. The height of these trees, coupled with their huge leaf expanse, has proved beneficial to several species of endangered mammals and birds. Scientists are predicting a substantial increase in numbers of some of the most vulnerable of these creatures - including certain species of butterfly and moth. Recent studies, however, have failed to throw any light on to the origin of these wonderful specimens."

Olivia listened, a conspiratorial grin lifting the corners of her mouth, her eyes sparkling with satisfaction. They had succeeded. She had not set eyes on Morgar or his frolic of fairies since the night that both she and a small group of fairies had traversed the universe, nearly a year ago, to extract pollen from the bloom of the huge Elephant Ear plant. It had been an attempt to save Bora the wind, whose lungs were saturated with carbon dioxide, as well as both the human and fairy populations, from the effects of air pollution. The fairies had successfully fertilised the seed of a huge Boston Redwood tree with the pollen from the Elephant Ear plant, creating a colossal tree capable of cleansing the atmosphere of harmful gases. Olivia was ecstatic - their success was unquestionable – however, something that the news reader had said caused her euphoria to subside. Olivia had crossed hostile plains, fought an army of ants and survived a tornado in an attempt to create this tree with the fairies. She had also been to the land where rainbows are born and witnessed the birth of a rainbow, but now, if the news reader was correct, rainbows were possibly extinct. This could not be happening!

Olivia went to bed that night with more on her mind than usual. The past year had flown by and she had all but forgotten the time that she had shared with the frolic of fairies. Her help had been enlisted when the frolic that lived at the bottom of her garden had become unwell. Their wings had suffered – perforations had appeared in them caused by the large amounts of carbon dioxide in the air- so they had sought Olivia's help, suspecting that the poisonous gas was man-made and that perhaps she could shed some light on achieving its elimination. Their journey had been hazardous but successful, culminating in the plantations that were now springing up in the rain forests of the Amazon and over vast fertile plains in India. But had realising their dream of a cleaner environment somehow destroyed the rainbow?

Not being able to sleep, Olivia got out of bed and went to stand by her bedroom window. She was greeted by a dazzling spectacle in her own back garden, that at first she could not comprehend. The base of the old oak tree was illuminated by what seemed to be dozens of tiny lights. Lights that were brighter than any household bulb or fluorescent strip and they seemed to move and sway in the cool night breeze. In an instant Olivia realised what the lights were. The bright lights were the fairies for, as Olivia had learnt a year ago, fairies create an aura which distinguishes them from one another. Each mother and infant are bonded by the creation of their own special bright light. A sudden fluttering at the window told Olivia that these small beings, whom she had grown to love, once again wanted something from her. Flinging wide the casement, Olivia passionately opened her world to the fairies.

"Olivia, Morgar has sent me to see if you would be willing to sit with us again, we have troubles that seem insurmountable."

Enya, one of the younger fairies that had befriended Olivia a year ago, seemed desperate for Olivia to join forces with the fairies once more.

"The body of Koh-i-Noor is pining for her heart. They have been separated for too long. She no longer throws out her arm to create a rainbow, a path down which she hopes her heart will return to her. Instead her light is fading – we fear that her light force may die if she is not reunited with her heart, the Koh-i-Noor diamond that is held captive in the Tower of London."

"Enya, you told me a year ago, as we watched the birth of a rainbow from the crevasse on the savannah beyond the rain forest, that you could not retrieve the Koh-i-Noor diamond from the Tower of London as it was guarded by dark powers - a force much stronger than your own."

"These powers date back to mystical times, Olivia, they are indeed dark and mischievous, but Olivia we have no choice, we must confront them and reunite the body of Koh-i-Noor with her heart or there will be no more rainbows."

Enya, a pretty blonde fairy with great sincerity and a true sense of purpose for one so small, now stood before Olivia wearing her own heart on her sleeve. She was passionate and brave, willing to risk all to retrieve the Koh-i-Noor diamond, which in its own right was shrouded by superstition and tagged with a curse. The stone that dates back to the Kakatiya dynasty was originally named Samantik Mani or Prince and Leader among diamonds. The magnificence of the diamond and its value symbolized the power of an empire, however, history has proved that whoever owns the Koh-i-Noor diamond has their life blighted by treachery, violence, torture and death.

"He who owns this diamond will own the world, but will also know all its misfortunes. Only God or a woman can wear it with impunity."

Olivia thought long and hard, for what lay ahead seemed so much more dangerous than simply creating a new species of tree to cleanse the atmosphere. What the fairies seemed to be asking of her this time was, in a word, unimaginable. However, having one's heart ripped out and held in a tower, as the body of Koh-i-Noor had, was also too hard to imagine or accept.

Olivia looked at her wall clock. Just before midnight. The expression in Enya's large, green, imploring eyes left Olivia with no choice.

"Enya, I will come to sit with Morgar and the frolic, I will listen to what you want from me."

The moment that Enya took her hand Olivia found herself being transported through the open window and down to the base of the oak tree. Familiar faces greeted her- Meta, a small feisty fairy, Brokk and Oberon, two male fairies – then Sorcha and Teagan, Enya's sisters, came to touch Olivia's hand in a gesture of friendship. Her heart then skipped a beat as Morgar came to sit next to her. She remembered the feelings that she always used to get when Morgar was close to her. Not fear exactly, nor embarrassment but an excitement that thrilled her emotions, for to her he seemed strong and handsome, someone in whom she was willing to entrust her life – although his whole being was, in some mystical way, totally alien to her.

Olivia remembered Nixie, a strange looking fairy with slanted eyes, who had at first intimidated her until she realised that Nixie had been infatuated with Morgar and had seen Olivia as a threat. Nixie was nowhere to be seen, which disappointed Olivia, who now remembered the terrible time when she and Nixie had been separated by Bora, the wind, whose rage had blown them through two different gates. Olivia had tumbled at great speed through the gate made from horn that made wishes come true whilst poor Nixie had been tossed through the gate made from ivory that made all dreams barren.

"Olivia, you have not changed, you are as beautiful as you were when we last met - if not more so."

Olivia blushed, letting her soft dark hair fall over her face, wisps dancing in the night breezes and tickling her pink cheeks.

"Olivia, has Enya told you what dangers we are to confront? We go into a time and space that we are not familiar with. We go with little more than determination and brave hearts. Are you prepared to join us again in our quest? We think that your help will be invaluable for we are sure, at times, that we will need your human presence. The curse of the Koh-I-Noor diamond may be coming to fruition - it may affect your world as well as our own."

There was no doubt that the seriousness of the mission scared Olivia, but the trust that she held for the fairies tempted her down a dark path from which she knew there might be no return.

"Morgar, tell me what has happened since the time that we witnessed the birth of a rainbow from that crevasse in the savannah beyond the Amazon rain forest?"

"As you know, Olivia, the body of Koh-i-Noor is a mass of diamond that no man has ever seen. It lies within the crevasse and it is indeed the birthplace of rainbows. It is so large that if any one man was to attempt ownership, it could be a destructive force with unimaginable power, far greater than the power of the heart that was wrenched from her and is now held within the walls of the Tower. That stone alone has been the downfall of dynasties, but Koh-i-Noor's light force is dying, she has been without her heart for centuries, she can withstand her loss no longer."

"Then we must reunite them, the body and the heart, for it seems that she has lost her soul along with her heart. Koh-i-Noor must become whole again for our world cannot and will not be the same without rainbows."

"Olivia, you are truly courageous. Our friend Mugwump, who you remember from the rain forest, is to join us - he travels from the Amazon as we speak and he will lead us in our quest, for he alone understands the body of Koh-i-Noor. We will leave tomorrow night at midnight, each carrying a Sheath of Coeval as we did on our last mission. The sheath, as you know Olivia, holds a shaft of pure white lanthanum metal with magic powers which will help to protect us from the dark mischief of the Tower - but remember they are not infallible, we must fight with cunning and valour if we are to return jubilant from our success."

Just as before, in the blink of an eye, Olivia found herself back to her normal size and tucked nicely into bed. The wall clock pointed to midnight and there was no sign that she had left her bedroom. It seemed unbelievable that she had just been as one with a frolic of fairies - but she knew from experience that she had, and that no one else would ever be any the wiser.

# CHAPTER 2
# Warriors of the Night

Mugwump traversed the universe crossing a well worn path through time and space surrounded by a capsule of bright light. The method of travel was as old as time itself; paths embossed into the hemispherical dome of the world were used by frolics of fairies who, like shooting stars, skidded with ease across night skies at light speed. His whole being had a sense of purpose and determination. The brown casaque that Mugwump wore bore witness to the reverence shown to the body of Koh-i-Noor, whose fate was now held in his hands and those of the frolic of fairies who awaited his arrival. His face, old and tired, showed no humour as he stepped out of the capsule. His dark brown coat fell so heavily that the night breezes failed in their attempt to billow it, as he made an exemplary entrance into Olivia's garden.

Morgar greeted him and, welcoming him into the glass house in which they had camped, made offerings of food and malmsey wine.

"Mugwump, we are pleased that you have enlisted our help to retrieve the Koh-i-Noor diamond from the Tower of London. The body of Koh-i-Noor must be reunited with her heart to save our magnificent rainbows. Her light force must not be allowed to expire."

"Morgar, it is good to hear your resolution in this matter, however you know only too well what we are up against. The Tower is a mystical place with many hidden dangers. Our foe is full of trickery - we have heard tales of mischievous spirits and sprites that would play games with us. The ravens too are not to be trusted for we have learnt that Erin and Neve, the two youngest ravens, have many tricks tucked under their wings. They are not malicious but impressionable and have been schooled by the sprites."

"The going will indeed be tough, Mugwump, but the task is not beyond us. We will go as one and with help from Olivia we can succeed."

"Olivia, you say, will she be entering the Tower by our side?"

"I have enlisted her help for I think that her human form may be invaluable to our endeavour. Have you an objection, Mugwump?"

"My reasoning would not be logical but I have a preference to leave her behind, the choice is however yours."

"Then my choice is that she joins us and with all my heart I know that she will not let us down."

"The decision is made then - we leave at midnight tomorrow so I think that now is the time for song and merriment, for we know not what the future may have in store for us."

Lights glowed brightly from the greenhouse at the bottom of Olivia's garden that night. No-one would see them, however, unless Olivia watched from her bedroom window. At three o'clock Olivia tossed fitfully in her bed and finally opened her eyes, seeing imaginary demons in the dark. Feeling hot and unsettled she left her bed and moved instinctively towards the window. She instantly caught sight of the tiny lights that flickered from her father's greenhouse and, knowing of Mugwump's intention to join the fairies on this mission, she longed to go down to the greenhouse to join in their discussions. She had never before gone to the fairies uninvited and was reluctant to do so now, but her curiosity had a will of its own.

Throwing on her jeans, she left the warmth and safety of her bedroom and tip-toed downstairs- her roll-neck sweater pulled up over her mouth as if in an attempt to silence her. She opened the living room door, which to her dismay, gave a warning squeal of alarm to the occupants of the home. She stopped in her tracks, holding her breath with fear and trepidation, however her escapade had so far gone undetected. Leaving the door ajar, she glided silently across the slippery wooden floor to the casement window. Lifting it just as far as need be, she slipped silently through it and out into the chilly, sweet smelling night air.

The pod that had been given to Olivia almost a year ago by Bardzak, the poet and scribe to many if not all frolics, had been mostly forgotten- put away in a drawer to gather dust during the past months. However as Olivia crept down the garden with the intention of going uninvited into the greenhouse, the pod suddenly appeared in front of her making her pulse race.

"Do you think it wise, Olivia, to inflict yourself upon the frolic at this late hour?"

The pod, which Olivia had been told contained wisdom, startled her into ill humour.

"Pod, I thought you were pushed to the back of a drawer! Why bother me now?"

The pod, aptly named because of its pea pod shape, did indeed contain wisdom and when Olivia had found herself in need of advice on her last journey with the fairies she had been most grateful for its help. This evening, however, she found the pod annoying having caught her creeping towards the greenhouse uninvited.

"Bother me now, bother me now?" The pod's voice rose in indignation.

The pod's discerning nature took umbrage at Olivia's tone and it shot straight back into her pocket where it had a habit of retreating to in times of strife.

"Oh Pod, do come out, perhaps I do need you after all."

The pod swiftly returned and hovered in front of Olivia's face, the green hues of his case changing shades as if with his mood swings. Warm shades of green interspersed with hot shades of a colour for which there was no name, for as Olivia had learnt, this pod seemed from a different world, possessing colours never before seen.

"Pod, what do you think that they are talking about? Do you think that Mugwump will dissuade the frolic from taking me with them? He was reluctant to take me on the last mission across the savannah."

"Would it be wise to be caught spying on them, Olivia? They may think that you are in cahoots with the sprites of the Tower."

"Oh, Morgar would not think that of me – would he?"

"One never knows, but if you ask me it would not be wise to put him to the test!"

Too late, a twig broke underfoot and they were discovered. Morgar fluttered out of the greenhouse to confront Olivia.

"Olivia, we were not expecting to see you until midnight tomorrow. Is anything wrong?"

"Morgar, I'm sorry, I woke and saw the lights in the greenhouse."

"Green house you say? The glass house is not green."

Olivia burst into floods of nervous laughter at Morgar's remark.

"Do you think it wise to laugh quite so loudly?" barked the pod.

Olivia quietened down and looked nervously at Morgar to interpret his reaction to her outburst.

"Morgar, I am sorry, you are right, the glass is not green but we do call this glass house a greenhouse for we raise green seedlings and saplings in it, the glass protects the new growth from the weather."

Morgar saw the funny side of their misunderstanding and smiled broadly. The pod relaxed and Olivia was invited into her father's glass house where the frolic of fairies were, for the want of a better word, squatting.

Once with the fairies Olivia instantly took on their shape and form, with the exception of the wings. This happened each time she was with them, it happened instantly without notice or feeling, and Olivia had become used to it. The pod nestled quietly back into Olivia's pocket and the introductions began.

"Olivia, you remember Mugwump?"

Mugwump came to stand before Olivia, taking her hand in his and touching his nose to hers. She thought this strange behaviour but Morgar's reassuring look put her at ease. Although the Mugwump's look was not appealing - he was old and fat, ill humoured at times - Olivia found that his breath was intoxicating, sweet almost floral; it sent mixed messages to her senses and she swayed slightly.

"It's a familiar greeting amongst the fairies of the Amazon. You will notice other forms of greetings from different frolics. You have not met Freya, she is from a frolic that lives in Ireland. Nixie is now with that frolic and Freya has come to join us," Morgar explained.

Freya, the most beautiful fairy that Olivia had ever seen, now stood before her extending her hand. Olivia took her tiny cold hand, at which point the fairy pulled Olivia towards her and almost in the blink of an eye flapped her wings forward to envelop Olivia briefly. The manoeuvre lasted a split second but slightly alarmed Olivia who felt the chill night air rush along her spine. Again a reassuring smile from Morgar kept Olivia from fleeing from these strange fascinating beings.

"We are going to make music Olivia, will you stay to play games and drink some wine with us?"

"Thank you, Morgar, I would love to."

Olivia watched a couple of the male fairies play what looked like a board game drawn out in the dust. The game, Nine Men's Morris, was a game similar to draughts where you have to make a line of three men (small round seed cases) or block your opponent from doing so. Others made music with unimaginable instruments made from reeds, nut shells and an assortment of debris discarded by humans that had been shaped into pipes and horns.

The music was mesmerising, haunting, leaving Olivia relaxed and comfortable. The fairies chatted and groomed themselves, something that Olivia had witnessed before. Whilst grooming, the fairies seemed to resemble insects in their habits, the females especially, pulling their wings forward and smoothing the soft down that covered both their wings and their shoulders. Olivia studied them with fascination, her eyes habitually returning to Freya for she was so beautiful.

She watched as Morgar went to stand by Freya and a pang of

jealousy ran through her body. This had to be kept in check, Olivia thought, as she reunited herself with Meta, a spirited fairy who had befriended her in the past. She averted her eyes from Morgar and Freya, concentrating instead on her father's greenhouse, for never before had she seen it from ground level. Everything was huge. The smells from the plants and the compost were delightful and enhanced due to their size, the bugs were as tall as her waist and she screamed as a wood beetle ran past her foot, knocking into her knee.

"Is it wise to scream so?" The pod chastised Olivia as he rushed from her pocket, embarrassing her until her cheeks flushed in the moonlight.

All attention was now on her and she wished with all her being that she was back in her bedroom.

"Olivia, we have asked you to join us on a dangerous mission. You will be carrying a Sheath of Coeval that may save you from harm. Once again we put our trust in you for you have already proven both your courage and your loyalty. Can we depend upon you once more?"

Olivia was slightly disappointed that Morgar had asked this question, for she had thought that both he and the frolic knew the answer, but when she affirmed her determination to retrieve the Koh-i-Noor diamond from the Tower of London, she was not disappointed by their reaction.

Cheers went up and each fairy that was to go on this mission, five in total, came to stand by her to show their allegiance and their delight in having her as part of their team. They got physically closer to Olivia than ever before, with their own peculiar caress or gesture, making her more familiar with the fairies than she had been in the past. They left a scent on her that she did not recognise, it was fresh, earthy and wonderful - an infusion of nocturnal aromas that stayed with her, enveloping her in comfort. Back in her own bed that night her mind would not rest. She could not wait for the next time that she would be with the fairies. She did not have long to wait, for at midnight the next day she would be embarking on an adventure that would last for who knew how long, or how dangerous it would be, but she would be with her beloved fairies - and her parents would be none the wiser.

# CHAPTER 3
## The Ravenmaster

"Emmets and Grockles," the two ravens sniggered, "Emmets and Grockles." They complained about the hordes of tourists who, like a swarm of ants, moved as one milling mass flowing onto their turf like an incoming tide.

"Where are the sprites? Come on, you sprites!" Erin taunted, in search of a distraction.

The two young ravens, Erin and Neve, strutted comically on Tower Green, one wing hanging slightly lower than the other, having had their lifting feathers trimmed by the Ravenmaster to prevent an aerial escape.

"Biscuits and blood," cawed Erin as her hunger grew, pinching at the lining of her stomach.

The Ravenmaster fed his ravens daily on raw meat and bird biscuits soaked in blood, however as feeding time approached, Erin suspected that her meal was not forthcoming for her master was nowhere to be seen.

"Biscuits and blood," Neve's beak opened hungrily as she too joined in with the loud demanding caws, their appetite making the birds cranky.

Suddenly their attention was caught by a shadow-like movement on an old stone wall to their left. At first their interest was short lived but, as the movement persisted and intensified, the ravens became instantly alert.

"Sprites," cawed Erin, unfolding her wings and holding them high to balance herself, half running and half hopping, in a most comical way towards the wall - Neve following closely behind. The two large birds hopped up onto the wall cawing loudly, waving their shiny lop-sided wings, drawing much attention to themselves from the public. The sprites were no more than thin air but they made the trees shake their boughs and rustle their leaves and they blew the ravens' feathers up to expose pink flesh. The ravens flapped their wings vigorously in protest, causing them to tiptoe as the turbulence threatened to have them airborne.

Sprites were known to be pestilent and they knew that the ravens were an easy target. They toyed with the ravens, tapping them on the beak then pulling at their tail feathers making them dance like clowns whilst the children laughed at their antics, unaware of their tormenters. Grog, an elderly raven, had been spirited away into thin air by the sprites, leaving the Ravenmaster bereft. Grog was eventually spotted on the roof of an East End pub called the Rose and Punchbowl but he never returned to the Tower, even though it had been his home for some twenty- one years. He obviously wanted nothing more to do with the sprites that had, in bygone times, taken up residence in the Tower. The cold stone rooms and corridors of the ancient buildings within The Tower walls provided a perfect playground for the infamous spectres that refused to be evicted.

Thor, however, a younger, brighter Raven, had an uncanny knack for mimicry. Not only could he repeat things that the Ravenmaster said, causing uproar amongst the Tower staff, but he also had very acute hearing and could tune into the sprites – for although sprites could not be heard by humans, they were in fact just thin air - Thor could sense their presence and pick up their communications which by instinct he could interpret. Have you ever had something disappear into thin air or seen bright blue or white dots of light when you have tightly closed your eyes then held them shut? Well, if the answer is yes - you have more than likely been visited by sprites - but they could not catch Thor out or tease him successfully as they did the other ravens and for this reason they left him alone, to pick on the less intelligent birds.

Unbeknown to Erin and Neve, the Ravenmaster watched his two ravens as they bounced and dodged on the ancient wall on Tower Green, pecking into the air, trying to spar with the sprites.

"Mischief," the Ravenmaster whispered to himself as he studied his ravens behaviour, for he was not unfamiliar with the sprites.

"Mischief," repeated Thor who stood close to his master.

The Ravenmaster looked down onto Thor grinning at the accurate mimicry of his own voice, wondering if it was indeed mimicry or if Thor shared his opinion of the sprites, that they were simply mischief personified. The Ravenmaster knew all too well that the sprite's mischief was not always playful. They could be spiteful, dangerous entities and were not to be messed with. He was suddenly engulfed by a sense of foreboding, for the sprites were uncommon visitors these days. Something had caused their reappearance and it did not bode well for the Tower.

The Ravenmaster watched as one child lost her ice cream from its cone and began to cry. Another child got dust in her eyes after a freak gust of wind seemed to lift the dirt and throw it straight into the girl's face, causing her to shelter in her mother's arms. Suddenly the happy atmosphere on Tower Green was lost, changing from one of laughter and frivolity to one of mischief and chaos, and the Ravenmaster knew why. Sprites!

The Ravenmaster left the concealed niche from where he had observed the behaviour of his ravens and strode purposefully forward with Thor hopping at his side. He knew that Thor would instinctively intimidate the sprites and stop their persistent attack on Erin and Neve, whose clowning antics were making them look stupid.

The Ravenmaster stopped short of his birds as swirls of wind carrying grit and debris flew up before him, stinging his eyes and scratching at his face. Onlookers stopped laughing and watched in horror as the Ravenmaster was temporarily blinded. Thor spread his wings and charged forward, his cawing so loud that it began to scare the children, whose parents retreated to protect their offspring. Soon Tower Green was empty - no tourist remained to see Thor charge time and time again pecking viciously into thin air, his voice a roar carried on Bora, the wind, whose mood was as truculent as his own.

As quickly as it had begun, Bora the wind subsided and the green seemed to return to normality. Thor stood by Erin and Neve, his chest feathers puffed out, his black eyes ever watchful darting here and there, but the sprites had gone. The Ravenmaster, a look of extreme concern puckering his face, herded his birds forward toward their cages.

"Good boy Thor, come and get your food."

"Good boy Thor," the bird repeated as he hopped, head held high, towards his pen.

The birds were well fed on the Ravenmaster's own mix of bird biscuits soaked in blood and some raw meat. They then settled down to relax, the set to with the sprites forgotten as their full stomachs made them sleepy. They groomed their feathers and dozed on their perches, oblivious to the ever present threat that surrounded them in walls, under foot and in the air itself.

The sprites gloated, waiting for the opportunity to rid the Tower of the ravens who were, in their opinion, a total waste of space. The sprites, however, totally underestimated the power of Thor who, with the fairies by his side, was to become their nemesis.

Soon darkness fell over The Tower as it did over Olivia's garden. Tiny lights appeared in her garden once more confirming the presence of the fairies. Olivia knew that no-one could see the lights except for her which filled her with an overwhelming sense of privilege. Her knowledge of the fairies' habits and customs, however, was still vague even though she had spent quite some time with them. For instance, she did not know if the fairies lived in dwellings of their own or hid in peoples' sheds or greenhouses for warmth. She had never had the courage to ask too many questions, for fear of seeming inquisitive. However, tonight, as she gazed longingly out of her bedroom window, her curiosity was aroused as the tiny fairy lights seemed to be spread out across the garden high in the trees. She longed to know all there was to know about her tiny friends, but knew that she must not leave her house to be with them until midnight.

A fluttering at her window startled Olivia out of her day dream. Enya was begging entry into Olivia's world, with some urgency.

"Olivia, Morgar has sent me to check that you are ready for our mission. Mugwump is complaining about your part in the dangerous task that lies before us but Morgar stands by you as guarantor. Olivia, I too will stand by you at all times, do not be afraid for we will carry our Sheaths of Coeval and we shall succeed."

Olivia felt mixed emotions - her courage grew in the knowledge that both Enya and Morgar were certain that her place in the team would be invaluable, but Mugwump's reluctance to include her cast shadows of doubts racing across her mind.

"Enya, I can only do my best to help this mission succeed."

"Come, do not look downcast. Mugwump has grown old and has lost his sense of adventure. We will surf the night sky, dance with Bora the wind, fight as one fearsome frolic and return with the Koh-i-Noor diamond, having outwitted the sprites and demons of The Tower."

Enya flew round Olivia's bedroom like some swashbuckling pirate slashing at imaginary enemies with an invisible sword, to the delight of Olivia who collapsed onto her bed in fits of laughter.

Enya was exceedingly pleased with her display and the effect it had had on Olivia who, pink- cheeked, rolled on her bed clasping a make-believe sword which protruded from her stomach.

When the peals of laughter subsided, the two became serious once more.

"Olivia, you must try to rest before joining us at midnight. You will need all of your strength for we do not know how long we will be gone. After retrieving the Koh-i-Noor diamond from The Tower of London we must reunite her heart with The Body of Koh-i-Noor. Our journey will be long and arduous."

Olivia felt a true sense of camaraderie with Enya, the tiny

fairy that she had saved a year ago from a spider's web in her father's potting shed. Enya hovered, then settled next to Olivia on the bed.

"This bed is quite obviously a very nice bed, but who keeps you safe and warm at night Olivia, do you sleep alone?"

Olivia thought this a very strange question and did not know how to answer it.

"People usually sleep alone until they get married Enya, then they sleep with their partner."

"Married, what is that Olivia?"

"Well, when two grown-up people fall in love - they get married. It means that they want to spend the rest of their lives together and they sign a sort of contract that says so, a marriage certificate."

"I see, you do not have a bright light that binds you together with your chosen one for all eternity, you have a certificate!"

Olivia felt all the romance of marriage evaporate, for a certificate sounded so dull in comparison to an all- consuming bright light.

"Enya, can I ask you a question?"

"Of course, what do you want to know?"

"Well, Enya, I was wondering where exactly you live, how do you keep warm? The nights must be so cold, living alongside the birds and the bees."

Enya looked concerned, thoughtful, as though she was contemplating whether or not to let Olivia into a secret.

"Olivia, humans do not know our habits for a reason. We live worlds apart, our species come together only under exceptional circumstances. You are exceptional, Olivia - we have put our trust in you and you have not let us down. I will tell you things that no other human has heard, you will witness our ceremonies, you have already seen our rekindling ceremony, and you will learn of our customs. They are ritualistic, involving all aspects of nature – but now you must rest; we will meet again at midnight."

Enya was gone.

# CHAPTER 4
## My Lady Jane

The moon was an opaque globe, her serenity stealing the beauty of the cloudless night sky as she held herself motionless for all to see. Olivia had left the safety of her home to meet with the frolic of fairies who were to be her guardians and fellow warriors for as long as it took to retrieve the Koh-i-Noor diamond and to reunite it with The Body of Koh-i-Noor, an unimaginably large mass of diamond which lay in a crevasse on a savannah far, far away.

Six warriors left Olivia's garden that night on a mission that seemed almost impossible. As usual, once in the company of the fairies, Olivia found herself the same size as them and she took up her Sheath of Coeval with pride, as did the fairies. Her comrades were Morgar, Mugwump, Enya, Freya and Brokk. Olivia found herself slightly uncomfortable in the company of Freya, for she could not take her eyes off the most beautiful fairy that she had ever come to know. Freya was quiet, assuming her role as warrior with a dignity and calmness that Olivia found quite lacking in herself.

Soon a bright light encapsulated them, bringing them close together as they were transported, by the pure energy of the fairies' light force, from Olivia's garden to The Tower of London, to commence their most dangerous escapade. Olivia found herself pressed closely against Freya and the smell was intoxicating; a glorious floral aroma that made Olivia breathe deeply. Freya's wings were held closely about her but a slight vibration, sounding like crumpling tissue paper, coming from them made Olivia wonder if she was indeed as tranquil as her persona suggested.

By the time the outline of the Tower could be seen protruding from the empty, grey streets of London, morning had dawned colouring the city blood red. What was the saying, Olivia thought to herself – red sky at night shepherds' delight, red sky in the morning shepherds' warning. Was this fierce red glow a warning of things to come?

Birds singing their dawn chorus could be seen crossing the Thames and flocking over Tower Bridge, but the ravens on Tower Green perched in ominous silence. The frolic of fairies stood on a low wall inside The Tower walls surveying the scene in front of them. Tall slate-coloured buildings jutted narrowly upwards looking cold, bleak and uninviting against the heat of the early morning sky. However, the glass memorial to those executed on Tower Green took on the crimson glow of the heavens.

"Gentle visitor pause awhile – where you stand death cut away the light of many days – here jewelled names were broken from the vivid thread of life – may they rest in peace while we walk the generations around their strife and courage – under these restless skies"

The words caused all to pause, each with their own thoughts, morbid or otherwise – all were silent.

With an unexpected suddenness the red sky changed, the surrounding temperature dropped as grey and black clouds scudded up the steely cold waters of the Thames towards The Tower. A wind whipped across the green, tossing leaves and litter into a swirling hotchpotch of debris. It was a mischievous air that scuttled through gates, doorways, up alleyways and in and out of windows. The frolic were caught off guard as the wind, Bora, blew this way and that, eventually separating them, herding them in different directions - the sprites were in charge and loving it!

Olivia felt a tingling loss of consciousness as her knees buckled beneath her. She was only faintly aware of blue and white lights dancing behind her closed lids, a bruising pain that covered most of her body and a feeling of travelling through the air. A heavy thud left her in a heap on a cold stone floor. Consciousness was a long time coming but when her senses finally returned to her, her whereabouts were difficult to take in. She found herself in a dark cold room furnished with heavily carved oak chairs, a table and a coffer. An ugly black writing desk stood in one corner looking as though it had been borrowed from an ancient church, an open book lay on top of it, perhaps a bible. The floor was stone as were the walls, leaving Olivia chilled to the bone even though a small fire crackled in the hearth. The windows were glazed with bubbled uneven glass providing poor visibility, showing the trees and the tower beyond disfigured through the ancient dusty casement.

Olivia rubbed her eyes, trying to make sense of what had just happened and wondered where her comrades were. Voices from an adjoining room filled her with trepidation.

"Lad, have they sent you for my lady's comfort?"

A kind- looking woman in a long grey dress with white apron and hat spoke to Olivia with a gentle voice.

Olivia turned looking for the boy to whom the woman spoke but there was no other person in the room. Olivia smiled in confusion as the woman approached to help Olivia to her feet.

"Come, my Lady Jane will welcome your company, young sir."

Olivia soon realised that she was back to normal size and that the fairies were nowhere to be seen. A tingle of fear ran up her spine for she sensed that all was not well. For instance, why did this woman apparently think that she was a boy?

"Sir, you have strange apparel, who has sent you to me, was it my husband?"

A young girl of maybe fifteen or sixteen came from the other room to stand before Olivia. She seemed to glide with an unearthly motion that had Olivia mesmerised. Her hair was bright red and she was dressed in shades of green and white, she looked to Olivia as if she had just stepped out of a history book.

"Are you in fancy dress?" Olivia whispered, in awe of this beautiful, composed young woman.

The girl laughed loudly as she slowly walked around Olivia studying her jeans and sweater.

"Boy, you jest, for it is you who are comically attired. Who has sent you and for what purpose – did my husband Lord Dudley perhaps dictate a message for me?"

Her intelligent hopeful eyes were not those that one would want to disappoint.

"Jane, my lady, do not wait for a tender word, they have betrayed you. To grieve so is as futile as to wish upon a star," said the nurse.

Lady Jane's eyes filled with tears and her nurse comforted her. Olivia's confusion was not to be clarified in the near future, for the scene that played out before her was as uncommon to Olivia as would be a scene from a Shakespearian play.

The nurse, who had been with Jane since infancy and had only good intentions, knelt before her ward and spoke again.

"Jane, you are queen, you must not be intimidated or influenced, this confinement will soon be undone, stand tall for you shall have your throne. Were the Crown Jewels not put before you for your pleasure this very morning?"

"They were, Madam, but I seek no pleasure in diamonds or rubies. I want Guildford to hear my words of devotion – for I do love him most truly, he is not the traitor that you would have me believe, it is our families who have plotted and forecast our destiny for their own purpose, he is my beloved husband."

The nurse flounced out of the room, leaving Olivia and the young woman who was said to be queen.

Silence made Olivia conscious of her own lack of identity in these unfamiliar rooms inhabited by strange people who seemed to be from another era. A sudden fleeting thought left Olivia in a state of disbelief. Perhaps this was another era and she had been separated from the fairies and from life as she knew it - indefinitely.

"Excuse me," Olivia managed to speak but with great difficulty, for her prior commitment to retrieving the Koh-i-Noor diamond with determination and valour was diminishing by the minute.

"Could you tell me the date, please?"

"What a question, it is 11th July, why do you ask, boy?"

"And what year would this be?" Olivia's mouth went dry, anticipating the worst.

"Why, the year is 1553, of course."

Jane, or whoever she was, stood before Olivia. Her dress, which fell to her feet, revealed raised wooden shoes that added three inches to her height.

"Do you stare at my ankles, boy, you are impertinent!"

"No, no," Olivia hurriedly replied, "I was looking at your shoes."

"What interest do you have in my chopines?" Jane closed in on Olivia, studying her clothes with renewed interest, especially the Sheath of Coeval that was clasped in Olivia's hand.

"What is your name and who sent you to me, is that a sword clasped in your hand, would you fight for my honour?" Jane smiled almost teasingly.

"My name is Olivia, I come on an errand."

Olivia could think of no other reply and wished that she could instantly evaporate.

"Olivia, you say? Do you come from Lord Dudley, is he well?" Jane's anticipation of a positive answer made it difficult to respond.

"I do not come from Lord Dudley, I come on a mission to retrieve the Koh-i-Noor diamond and return it to its rightful owner or there will be no more rainbows."

Olivia realised how this must sound and searched the room frantically for a means of escape, but with brow perspiring, she found there was none.

"What mischief are you about, sir?" Jane was now as confused as Olivia and seemed slightly irritated.

Mischief, Olivia thought. The sprites - she realised now that she had been sent back in time, to a barbaric era where people were beheaded on Tower Green. Her knowledge of history was not good but she was beginning to understand that she was indeed talking to Lady Jane Grey, Queen for Nine Days, in the year 1553. This was not good, for she knew the outcome of this historic tragedy.

Olivia spent the best part of an hour explaining herself to the bemused Queen of England, who sat quietly as she listened with interest to Olivia's story. Superstition played a large part in the beliefs of people of this time, so Olivia played on Jane's fascination with mystical happenings and painted a vivid picture; however, all Jane was really interested in was her beloved Lord Dudley.

Jane's mind seemed to wander as she gazed distractedly out of the warped casement window, the view as unclear as her precarious future.

"Koh-i-Noor diamond, you say, Olivia? I have not heard of such a gem, nurse; bring us some sweetmeats if you please."

"Pod," Olivia whispered earnestly behind the sleeve of her jumper so as not to attract Jane's attention.

"Pod, I need your help."

"Would it be wise, Olivia, to startle the Queen of England with the presence of a hovering pod?"

"Pod, don't mess with me. Why does Jane not know of the Koh-i-Noor diamond?"

"Olivia, it would be wise for you to pay attention in your history lessons. The Koh-i-Noor diamond did not become part of the Crown Jewels until the nineteenth century - you are currently residing in the sixteenth century!"

"Pod, we must get back to the others. Where are they?"

"At present it would not be wise to join them. They have problems of their own to contend with. Would it not be wise to simply console the sweet lady who sits beside you, before she faces her untimely demise?"

Olivia, whilst sharing a plate of sugary sweetmeats with the queen, felt suddenly humbled, knowing what this innocent young girl was to face in the near future.

"Jane, can I help you in some way before I leave?" Olivia asked with true sincerity.

"Olivia, you are a strange young thing, what is it that you think you could do for me?"

Olivia thought long and hard, then gave Jane an answer that brightened her pretty face.

"I could get a message to your husband, Guildford Dudley, if it would please you."

"Olivia, there is nothing that would please me more, for he thinks that my devotion to him no longer exists; however, we are but innocent pawns amongst scheming families. I want him to know that my forgiveness is wholehearted and that my vows to him are still true."

"I shall do it, Jane, I shall go to him now and he will know that you have not deserted him."

"I know not who you are or where you have come from, Olivia, you seem not of this world, but if you can succeed in this quest I will be forever in your debt. I will face my destiny with courage knowing that Dudley is certain of my devotion and that we will be reunited in heaven, if not on earth."

The young queen, who was to be sovereign for so short a time, kissed Olivia on the cheek before Olivia left the oppressive gloom of Jane's confinement through a heavy oak door held open by the nurse. She headed straight for the Beauchamp Tower where Dudley and his brothers were being held.

There were no guards outside the tower so Olivia raced up the cold stone stairwell but all was not well. A pulling feeling in her head made her queasy and unsteady on her feet.

"Pod, what is happening to me?"

"The sprites are toying with you; it would be wise to make haste and fulfil your promise to Jane," said the pod, a deep sense of concern in his voice.

Olivia looked inside the room at the top of the stairwell. Several men sat around talking and playing a game with coins in the dirt on the floor. She recognised Dudley by the white and gold suit that Jane had described so vividly.

"Dudley - Guildford Dudley?" Olivia shouted, but there was no response.

"Pod, my ears are ringing, my hands are trembling and nobody can hear me."

"Olivia, they cannot see or hear you, you must make a sign. Take your sheath Olivia, quickly, hold it up and carve a sign into the wall, do you see the graffiti that others have left?"

With a great effort Olivia lifted The Sheath of Coeval and pointed it towards the wall beside Dudley, her strength had all but left her but as she focussed her mind's eye down the shaft of her weapon, she experienced the power of the sheath for the first time as she carved the name "Jane" into the stone wall beside Dudley. Before her vision was lost and she gave in to her imminent plight, she saw the heart- wrenching expression on Guildford Dudley's face. As he touched the wall with trembling hand, a tear rolled across his cheek- his beloved Jane, who as history tells was later to be beheaded on Tower Green, had not abandoned him.

# CHAPTER 5
# Dark Mischief

The pulling feeling in Olivia's head intensified until she found herself plunged into darkness; thrown skyward, then tossed to the ground – thick, damp grass cushioning her fall. A huge black bird loomed over her, spreading his wings and cawing so loudly that Olivia let out a shrill scream that brought Pod from his safe place in Olivia's trouser pocket.

"Would it be wise to scream so, Olivia? You will draw attention to us and Thor's intentions are most honourable. He is familiar with the sprites and has a desire for revenge. The sprites torment the ravens of the Tower but Thor is a worthy adversary."

Pod hovered in front of Thor, the wisest and most cunning of the ravens that inhabited the grounds of the Tower. Thor pecked into the air excitedly, trying to catch the pod which ducked and dived playing the raven's game with enthusiasm.

"Pod, where are the fairies, are they safe?" Olivia momentarily forgot the pain of her own bruises, concern for the fairies numbing her discomfort and making her impatient with the antics of Pod and Thor. She realised that her size was once again the same as the fairies, which meant that they must be close.

Looking upwards, to her dismay she saw a sight that filled her with fear. Each fairy hung suspended by web attached to a flagpole high over Olivia's head. The only thing that prevented them from being invisible behind the mesh of web was the constant fluttering of their wings. Bora, the wind, screamed in anguish: his violent temper, aimed at the sprites, blew the fairies this way and that as he whipped up a storm to vent his anger.

"Pod," screamed Olivia. "Look above you!"

Thor was the first to see what the sprites had done, although his flightless wings prevented him from helping the fairies, suspended as they were in cocoons of cobweb, which to fairies was an irritant with adverse effects. Something in the webs of spiders, maybe an enzyme, had an unfortunate effect on the wings of fairies, rendering them temporarily flightless and leaving them vulnerable to attack.

"Olivia, The Sheath of Coeval, you must use it again – hurry!" shouted the pod.

Olivia stood, but Bora the wind nearly knocked her feet from under her in his fury. She steadied herself, raising The Sheath of Coeval in front of her and, aiming it high at the tangle of web that had the fairies suspended, she once again focussed her mind's eye on the sheath and with a determined swish, she severed the noose- like threads.

"That's magic!" Olivia whispered to herself as she watched the fairies plummet to the ground almost unscathed, although their wings were in need of immediate attention.

Morgar bellowed a curse at the invisible foe that had humiliated the fairies and robbed them of their sheaths, his voice startling Olivia who had just managed to compose herself.

After freeing himself from his cocoon of web, he came to stand by Olivia causing her face to flush by his closeness. He still filled her with awe and a sense of excitement when he was close, so when his wings encircled her, she was rendered both speechless and incapable of movement.

"Olivia, we thought we had lost you, but not only are you safely here in front of us, but you have also saved us from our - what shall I say, difficulty!"

She felt that she was being teased, but the events of the past few minutes and her voyage back in time to meet with a young queen who was to be beheaded, had left Olivia with no real sense of humour. A tear spilled from each eye and she hung her head in an attempt to hide her weakness, but it did not go unnoticed by Morgar.

"Olivia, you shed a tear, are you hurt?"

Olivia mumbled a negative response and hoped that Morgar would step back and give her space to breathe, but he did not.

"Olivia, I am sending you home. Enya can go with you. I cannot put you at further risk."

"No, please don't, I can help you – I just have, haven't I?"

"You have, Olivia, you have done well and you are a brave and resourceful girl, but we fairies have an indestructible element that humans do not possess. We were in no great danger hanging up there, the sprites were trying to make us look foolish, and they succeeded, did they not?"

Morgar laughed but with no real humour.

"I have learnt to use The Sheath of Coeval Morgar, I will be able to help, I promise I won't get into any more trouble, please don't send me home."

Morgar looked down into Olivia's determined eyes and his resolve weakened.

"Very well, Olivia, but from now on you must stay close by my side – we have not seen the worst yet."

As Morgar stepped back allowing Olivia to relax, she felt all eyes upon her. What were the other fairies thinking? Had Morgar stayed too close for too long or were they disappointed by his decision to let her stay? Olivia could not interpret their mood but she did not feel comfortable. Especially with Freya's large green eyes upon her, but it was Mugwump who unexpectedly put her at her ease.

"Olivia, let me thank you for your courage, I give you my casaque, here put it on, it will not only keep you warm but it will also protect you from any further mischief from the sprites. As Morgar says, we fairies were not in any great danger from the sprites, but you, my dear, may suffer a lethal blow."

Mugwump's unexpected act of chivalry left Olivia in a state of uncontrollable emotion for she had never felt that he, of all the fairies, approved of her company. He wrapped the long brown robe about her and she instantly felt its enchantment. It felt as if it had a life of its own which now controlled her movements, guiding her and protecting her. She was most grateful for the secure feeling of warmth and comfort that it gave her and so rewarded Mugwump with a kiss on his cheek.

Mugwump flinched and Olivia misread his reaction. She instantly regretted the foolish act and blushed in confusion, but looking at Morgar, who had the biggest grin on his face, she realised that she had not offended Mugwump but simply embarrassed him, for he was not used to acts of such kindness. His face, that was always so stern and disapproving, now glowed with a warm flush that the fairies had never seen before and it was causing some light- hearted nudging and teasing amongst them.

Mugwump, however, instantly regained composure and led the fairies and Olivia to a shaded nook where they would tend to their wings and forge a plan of action to retrieve the Koh-i-Noor diamond that had been imprisoned within The Tower walls for far too long.

Olivia watched as the fairies groomed themselves. It was a moment of relaxation for the frolic and Olivia watched spellbound. The fairies pulled their wings forward, smoothing down the skin of the wings which Olivia noticed was full of pulsating veins. Fine hair grew over their shoulders and down across their wings which still held some of the web that was so destructive to the fairies. Olivia reminisced about the first time that she had seen a fairy, the time that she had saved Enya, who had been caught in a web in her father's potting shed. She was roused from her reflective state by Freya who had walked over to stand next to her.

"Olivia, could you help me to get this web out, I can't reach the back of my shoulders?"

Olivia was flattered to be asked for help from Freya and instantly began to clean the web from Freya's back and wings. The skin of the wings was the softest skin that Olivia had ever felt, even though it showed signs of irritation and swelling through the soft wheat- coloured down. The pulsating veins, however, lying just under the skin were what caught Olivia's attention. You would expect veins to take on a bluish hue but the veins that Olivia now studied were filled with a myriad of spectacular colours that seemed to cascade down Freya's back, reflecting off and illuminating the wall behind them.

Olivia once again felt in awe of these tiny beings, realising just how little she knew about them. She had likened them in the past to humans, but realised now like never before, that they had nothing in common with humans at all. For the first time since she had met the fairies she felt a little afraid, unsure if she should be with them and unsure if she was safe, for seeing Freya in such detail made her realise now that they were not from her world at all, in fact they were an unknown, almost alien species.

"Olivia, you are trembling, are you all right?"

Olivia's face could not hide the fear she now felt and Freya looked concerned, unaware that Olivia's fear was focussed on her and her kind. Freya turned to face Olivia, wrapping the long brown casaque around her tightly, giving her a gentle hug at the same time.

"Olivia, you are an extraordinary human being, but all beings, be they fairy or human, feel fear at some time in their life. You are, however, safe with us – we would not let anything happen to you. See, you wear Mugwump's casaque," she tweaked the collar. "you wear it well, come now smile again with those beautiful red lips and we will be on our way. The Koh-i-Noor diamond is impatient!"

# CHAPTER 6
# The Wrath of Bora

The casaque hugged Olivia and, although she assumed it would be heavy to wear, it was in fact as light as a feather. It held her tightly, enabling her to glide effortlessly over the cobbled ground, following closely behind Morgar. The fairies had cleaned the web from their wings and eaten biscuits made from wheat and honey. The malmsey wine that they always had with them was made from pure nectar and sustained them for hours on end, it was delicious and Olivia, too, was grateful for its uplifting quality.

The bird named Thor strode out before them. His eyes, as black as jet, darted this way and that in nervous readiness for the appearance of the sprites, but as they crossed Tower Green towards the Waterloo Barracks where the crown jewels were displayed, they seemed for a time to pass unnoticed.

The stillness was, however, a prelude to a storm that was at that very moment being whipped up by the sprites of The Tower. As the fairies, led by Thor, traversed the ancient green, the tranquil autumnal skies seemed to erupt and change. The unpretentious grey clouds in the sky suddenly rolled, forming eerie black vapours silhouetted by a sinister shade of slate green. Thor threw up his wings cawing loudly, a sense of alarm spreading throughout the frolic. The wind, Bora, seemed to skate slowly at first across the grass, his aggression mounting with caution at first as he meandered through alleyways, rattled windows and blew debris up stairwells. Both Thor and the fairies picked up their pace as a feeling of impending disaster coursed through their veins. The sky seemed to close in on them as the inner square got darker and tourists ran for cover. A loud thunder clap announced the onset of the storm whilst the gods up above threw down a lightning bolt that hit the green like a javelin.

The sprites, intent on antagonising Bora, were having it all their own way as they danced before Thor's eyes with glee, leaving blind spots on his retinas. Thor ducked and dived trying to avoid the persistence of the sprites' torment, however he did not seem able to out- manoeuvre them and stumbled. Thor's wings jerked uncontrollably, hitting the ground and causing his back to arch skyward as his legs buckled beneath him. He looked to Olivia like a fallen animal in the throes of death, his movements out of control, panicked by the unknown and her heart went out to him, as she too began to panic.

Thor regained his footing just as huge hailstones started to cascade from above. He stood up and on tiptoe flapped his wings vigorously in front of him, his beak wide as he emitted an unearthly noise that dispersed even the most mischievous of sprites. Bora, the wind, by this time had whipped himself up into an uncontrollable frenzy blowing gale force gusts of wind across the green, ripping through hedges and breaking branches off trees. His anger was indiscriminate, ruthless and unremitting, impulsive and indestructible.

From a window high above, The Ravenmaster watched his birds as they were blown from their perches; Bora knew no mercy as one bird after another fell foul of his fury. The birds heroically tried to get to their cages where they could find a small amount of shelter but the weakest one, Erin, lost her footing and was thrown against a stone wall. She lay there motionless, losing both wing and tail feathers to the wind, Bora, who without conscience ravaged all who lay in his path. Morgar and Mugwump turned from their own trajectory to go to the aid of Erin, with Olivia, Freya, Enya and Brokk following closely behind.

At first inspection they thought that Erin had lost her life. She lay on her back, her scaly black legs pointing skyward with mud clogged beneath her claws where she had heroically clung to life. Her beak was open and Olivia could see a dark pointed tongue within, which had specks of blood on it. Her neck lay at what appeared to be a disjointed angle, suggesting that it had been broken. Olivia was unable to look any longer for her grief was making her weak and tearful and she did not want the frolic to think of her as vulnerable. Morgar, however, caught hold of her wrist and pulled her to the front of the group shouting her name over the noise from the storm.

"Olivia, work quickly for we must save Erin. You are the only one who has still got a Sheath of Coeval; you must use it now to save Erin."

Olivia looked confused but she instinctively drew the sheath forward, clasping it with both hands. She paused to look into Morgar's eyes, perhaps for guidance, but as she lifted the sheath she found that she needn't have faltered. A feeling from the pit of her stomach grew in intensity as she concentrated her mind's eye on the sheath and where it was pointed. She felt a sense of power run through her body as she drew the sheath over Erin's head then ran it over the full length of the fallen bird. Bright lights shot from the sheath, causing the hammering hailstones to hiss and melt. At first there was no response from Erin and an overwhelming sense of disappointment and failure filled Olivia's being. Then, unexpectedly, nothing more than a small sparkle of light pirouetted into Erin's black eyes, changing them from dull lifeless black beads to twinkling, winking orbs of life. Erin's claw-like feet twitched as strength coursed once more through her body, she flapped her wings vigorously as she got to her feet so quickly that the fairies and Olivia had to duck to protect themselves. Erin stood tall and shook out her feathers –what was left of them – then let out a joyous "cawwwwww!" The Ravenmaster looked on, a puzzled but relieved look ironing out the deep-set wrinkles of his troubled features.

The ravens, now safe, stood on the perches in their cages, all but Thor whose stance told the fairies that he was not done with the sprites. His feathers were held close against his body, his legs bent, lowering him close to the ground with head and neck pointing straight forward, the glare in his fierce black eyes a warning to all who crossed him.

Bora's temper calmed, clouds lifted, the gale subsided and the hail turned to a gentle rain. Bora could be seen changing the turbulent Thames back into a rippling passage for boats and ferries as he reduced his speed and rolled off down the river. The fairies, in a moment of comparative calm, could not help but notice that, although the sun now shone brightly through a curtain of sparkling rain, there was no sign of a rainbow.

The job that the fairies had come to do must now be done and done quickly for they feared that time was now against them. If the Koh-i-Noor diamond was not reunited with the body of Koh-i-Noor soon, she may yet expire.

The fairies re-grouped with Thor as their leader. They picked up their pace heading for the Waterloo Barracks. The loss of their Sheaths weighed heavily on the minds of the frolic for if they fell into the wrong hands, who knew what could happen. However, their path was now clear and the barracks up ahead looked, if not inviting, at least undisturbed by the activities of the sprites.

Their optimism, however, was short lived for as they left Thor guarding their rear and entered the barracks a foreboding sight greeted them. Their sheaths, taken against their will, hung suspended over the case which contained the precious Koh-i-Noor diamond for which they had come. The frolic stood, watching in total disbelief, at the formation of their sheaths that slowly rotated, suspended in mid air like a glinting star standing sentinel over the diamond. The sprites were again in charge.

"The Wizard's Foot," said Morgar, the words floating out of his mouth on an exhalation of defeat, his expression portraying the gravity of their situation.

"What do you mean, Wizard's Foot, Morgar?" asked Olivia, her anxiety making her voice low and earnest.

"You see the formation of the sheaths, Olivia: the five ends meeting in the middle and the five handles spread out to create a star effect. This is called The Wizard's Foot, it is invincible, and fairies are unable to go within five feet of it. The sprites have done their job well."

Mugwump pushed to the front and looked closely at the feat that had rendered their mission impossible.

"By The Sheath of Coeval," Mugwump hissed. "They have made the giddy goat out of us, have they not, Morgar?"

"They have played their monkey tricks with us, Mugwump, that's for sure. The question is - where do we go from here?"

Invisible to humans as they were, within the walls of The Waterloo Barracks, the frolic could now take their time to think of a solution to their quandary. They sat on the cold stone floor, each with their own thoughts on how to outwit the sprites. One suggestion after another by Brokk, Enya and Freya was dismissed until the group were morose and agitated. Suddenly Olivia leaped to her feet, a look of dismay contorting her features.

"Edward and Harry are over there, they will see me," Olivia wailed.

"Olivia, have you forgotten? You are also invisible when you are with us, neither your friends nor the other tourists in the building will be aware of your presence." Morgar sounded tired and distracted and Olivia cursed her own stupidity.

Regaining her composure, Olivia remembered that what Mogar had said was true. Her friends from school had obviously come to The Tower for a visit and were blissfully unaware that a friend of theirs was with a frolic of fairies in the middle of an extremely challenging mission. Olivia relaxed once more and re-joined the frolic in a moment of serious consideration. Suddenly Olivia had an idea.

"Pod, are you there? I need your help."

A shuffling from within Olivia's pocket announced the appearance of Pod, who hovered before her in his customary supercilious manner.

"Pod, The Sheaths of Coeval, they are above the Koh-i-Noor diamond. The sprites have made The Wizard's Foot from them, the fairies cannot go near."

"Would it be wise to raise your voice Olivia? Have you not

heard the saying that walls have ears? The saying is especially true here in the tower. The walls hold echoes too, not only from the past but also the present, listen and you will hear."

A chill ran up and down Olivia's spine, her eyes darted this way and that, for fear now made her jumpy. She needed a minute to regain her composure so she leant her head against the cold, hard wall of the barracks. She shut her eyes, letting the chill of the stone wall soothe her brow, but suddenly her eyes shot open when voices, as predicted by Pod, seemed to echo from within the walls themselves.

Olivia listened carefully. The voices were muted at first then became clear, recognisable and not at all alarming. The voices were those of Edward and Harry, echoing round the walls from where they were chatting on the other side of the glass case that held The Koh-i-Noor diamond. This gave Olivia an idea, but first she needed some valuable information from Pod.

"Pod, The Wizard's Foot, will it hurt me or just the fairies?"

"The Wizard's Foot is used in sorcery as a talisman or amulet against magic. It is said to represent the five senses, hearing, sight, smell, taste and touch. If you can breach the five sheaths using the five senses you will not only be safe, but capable of retrieving the sheaths and exposing the diamond, but beware, your hand may not be party to the retrieval of the sheaths, you must use the senses of a third party to do your bidding or The Wizard's Foot may yet grow horns." Although Olivia found Pod's words baffling, she knew that she alone had the best chance of retrieving the sheaths. She had no choice.

# CHAPTER 7
## The Flaming Heart

Olivia had not fully formed a plan when she separated herself from the frolic and slipped away from them. Her mind was made up - she would retrieve the sheaths and prove herself to the fairies once and for all. With Pod as her confidant she would somehow coerce her friends, Harry and Edward, into helping her, using their senses to solve the riddle and expose The Koh-i-Noor diamond.

As she rounded the corner and saw her friends in front of her she suddenly realised that she was still the size of a very small doll. This complicated matters. There was no way that she could communicate with her friends if she was the size of a fairy, not to mention invisible – or was there?

"Pod, do you think that we can succeed if my friends can't see or hear me?"

"They may not be able to see you, Olivia, but would it be wise to assume that they can't hear you?"

"Oh, this could be fun," thought Olivia.

"Harry, Harry, can you hear me?"

"Yes, who said that?" Harry spun round looking for who had called his name.

"Edward, did you hear someone call me?" In his confusion Harry looked comical and a little stupid.

This is going to be fun, thought Olivia, who had to suffocate a snigger. She knew that she would have to think quickly or the boys would lose interest.

"Hearing is the first sense Pod, if Harry can hear me, I'll simply ask him to take one of the sheaths down."

"Harry, could you reach one of those swords above your head for me, please, and place it on the ground?"

Harry looked up at the rotating sheaths and did exactly what was asked of him.

This is too easy, thought Olivia. The next sense would be sight, let's see what we can do with that, she mused.

"Edward, do you see the four rotating swords that are left? Could you reach one and put it next to Harry's one?"

Edward obeyed Olivia in the same way that Harry had - without question.

"Now, Harry," Olivia began, thinking her task was as good as done, but things took a turn for the worse as Mrs Curran, their mother, called the boys from the exit and the boys ran off.

"Boys have got the attention span of a worm," thought Olivia as they disappeared from sight, now what?

Three sheaths were left revolving over the case that held the Koh-i-Noor diamond, but with no-one left to help her Olivia felt frustrated and cross.

"Pod, we have failed, I have no other tricks up my sleeve."

"It would be wise to trust your senses, Olivia, listen – hear what you need to hear, see, smell, touch and taste, they are there in front of you."

Olivia had no idea what Pod was talking about and felt in need of a reprieve. Her head was spinning, so she sat once more on the cold stone floor and rested her back against the wall. The smell that seemed to waft in front of her nose was familiar but Olivia couldn't place it. She absent-mindedly slid her index finger down the wall feeling its dampness, then touched her finger to her tongue. Sweetmeats, that's what she could taste and smell, she remembered being with Jane, the queen who was ultimately to be beheaded, and she remembered the sugary sweetmeats that the nurse had given them to eat. Why were these senses so real to her now?

"Olivia." The word reverberated around the room, seeming to pass Olivia's ears time and time again.

"Olivia, my friend, I have come to repay my debt."

Olivia's mind spun with confused memories of her time with Jane, her thoughts tumbled this way and that, agitated by the continuous sound of the voice bouncing off the walls. Were the words in Olivia's mind swirling around or were they in the room or in the walls themselves? Olivia sank her head to the ground, tears streaming from her eyes, splashing onto the floor as she covered her ears with her hands. Things were happening that were beyond her imagination and fear overwhelmed her.

"Olivia, you have your swords, I did not forget you, I am at peace, Olivia, I am at peace."

The voice touched Olivia's ears like a soft whisper on a cold night. The room went quiet and a chill ran through Olivia, a chill that even Mugwump's casaque could not keep out. Her hands held tightly over her ears trembled and the tears ran freely. A last choking sob escaped from Olivia's mouth before she could once again open her eyes and face her demons. Alone on the floor she looked in disbelief at a pile of five sheaths before her.

Pod had retreated to his place in Olivia's pocket, leaving her time to dry her tears and compose herself. Before rejoining the frolic, she took a moment to consider what had just happened to her as her heart pounded with trepidation, rendering her temporarily impotent. Her achievement, however, was incredible and soon pride overcame her distress and she longed to tell Morgar that she had retrieved the sheaths. She collected the bundle and jubilantly retraced her steps to where she had left the frolic, by a pillar on the other side of the glass display cabinet. To her dismay they were nowhere to be seen, her smile faded, replaced by a worried frown. To add to her concern, in the blink of an eye, she found herself back to human size, which she knew meant that the fairies were not close by. The sheaths, now the size of large swords, became not only heavy to handle but also conspicuous, the writing and motifs on them making them look like historic relics that should be in one of the cabinets. This did not fit in with her plans and to make matters worse, she bumped into her close friend from school, Rosie.

"Olivia, you're not a member of the historic society, are you? What are you doing here?"

Olivia had forgotten about the day out to The Tower of London that had been arranged by her history teacher, and cursed her bad luck, to be here at The Tower with the fairies on the very same day that some of her school friends were here.

"What are you carrying, are they swords?" asked Rosie with her customary jovial smile.

"Rosie, how lovely to see you here, yes, umm, yes they're swords."

"Can I help you, where are you taking them?"

"Help me? Errr, no, no need Rosie, I'm just going, umm, over there!"

Olivia tried to point but lost her grip on the heavy sheaths, dropping them with an enormous clatter on to the floor, causing no end of speculation by the multi-national tourists, as to what this young girl was doing with a bunch of lethal- looking weapons.

"Rosie, yes, could you help me, here you take these two and I'll take the rest."

The girls picked up the sheaths and made a hasty exit, walking, almost running, to the green outside The White Tower where the ravens roamed freely, pecking absently at the grass. Olivia noticed Thor who was eying her with what looked like concern, although she wasn't sure.

"Rosie, lovely to see you, you'd best get back now before you're missed."

"Not until you tell me what you are up to, you look like you're having far more fun than me."

"Oh, I'm not, believe me, I'm err, just running an errand for someone."

"Well I'm not going until you tell me, I know you, Olivia, and you're up to something."

Rosie had a conspiratorial look in her eye which Olivia recognised. They were close friends and Olivia could not keep any secrets from Rosie.

"Rosie, I can't tell you what I'm doing; I'm not exactly supposed to be here. I don't want anyone else to see me, can I fill you in tomorrow - I'll phone you."

Rosie would not take no for an answer, however, and simply refused to leave Olivia's side until she had some answers. Olivia's brow began to perspire at the thought of the fairies finding her chatting to Rosie, who was now sticking to her like glue. Olivia then saw Enya astride Thor's back and went into an instant fit of apoplexy, causing her to stutter incoherently. Enya was sitting, legs hidden beneath black feathers, looking positively majestic on the back of the huge raven.

"Olivia, do you think that bird is looking at us, he's giving me quite an uncanny feeling," said Rosie who was beginning to think that all was not well.

Thor's head was low to the ground, staring at the two girls as if he were about to charge forward. Olivia, realising that this was a good opportunity to get rid of Rosie, played along with the drama.

"Rosie, you're right, that raven has an evil look in his eye, I think he is going to come after us, perhaps we had better get back inside, you should return to your group, go on now, I'll follow."

As if understanding what was going on, Thor crept forward, low to the ground, eyes and beak pointing at Rosie until she turned and fled back inside The Barracks.

Enya was in a fit of laughter astride the fearsome Thor who, acknowledging the fact that he had done a good job, let out a celebratory caw.

"Olivia, come, take my hand."

Enya flew to Olivia who, in the blink of an eye, reverted once more to the size of the fairies. Taking half of the sheaths each, Enya led Olivia back inside The Barracks to where the frolic had re-grouped. Neither Morgar nor Freya looked pleased when they saw Olivia triumphantly approaching, carrying her sheaths towards them, bent over by their weight and almost tangled and tripping in Mugwump's casaque. Their relief at her safety, however, outweighed their annoyance at her independent nature and they congratulated her on her success in retrieving the sheaths. Mugwump, against his better nature, gave Olivia a broad beaming smile that warmed her and relieved her of any reproachful thoughts she had of wrong doing, however Brokk seemed to remain distant.

"We must now achieve what we came here for," announced Mugwump. "we must exchange the real Koh-i-Noor diamond for The Misfit. I call it The Misfit in jest, for no living person will ever be any the wiser. For all eternity, people will recognise The Misfit as the real Koh-i-Noor diamond, there will be no trait to distinguish one from the other. The curse of the diamond, however, will die after reuniting The Body of Koh-i-Noor with her heart, therefore the human race should be grateful," Mugwump sent Olivia a significant glance.

The frolic gathered around the glass case that held the Koh-i-Noor diamond. Olivia could only stand by and watch at this point, Brokk insisting that she stay well back. The room was host to many tourists who stood on the conveyor belts that rambled along each side of the enormous glass display cabinets full of historic orbs, crowns and precious gems. Huge metal doors, designed to protect the jewels from theft, stood erect and impenetrable at each exit. Rosie and her group were at one end of the display, crouching whilst intent on drawing one of the exhibits. Rosie held her bottom lip between her teeth in an expression of deep concentration, making Olivia long to be with her friend and share her secret, but she knew that could not be.

Suddenly Olivia was mesmerised as she saw the frolic moving into formation above the Koh-i-Noor diamond. Unnerved by the look in Brokk's eyes when he had hovered past her to take his position, Olivia retreated to a safe distance from where she could only watch what was to happen next. She glanced over to Rosie again who, oblivious to what was taking place in the same room, chatted and laughed with her colleagues making Olivia feel unsettled, edgy and almost home-sick.

A noise drew Olivia's attention back to the frolic as they began to chant. They held their Sheaths of Coeval over their heads whilst hovering over the cabinet and, as the points of the sheaths touched the glass, sparks flew off into the air resembling sparks thrown from an anvil when a hammer strikes. There was no reaction from either the tourists or the Beef Eaters, who were there to answer questions, confirming that the exploits of the frolic were indeed invisible to the human eye.

This peacock's eye that shines so bright,
Must traverse the skies and the seas tonight,
Samantik Mani your eye is all seeing,
Your body awaits to become a whole being.

The chanting went on but Olivia could not interpret all the words, she did know however, that during one ancient dynasty the Koh-i-Noor diamond had been set as a peacock's eye on a magnificent throne and assumed that this was what the chanting referred to. Eventually she saw the stone rise from the crown into which it was set. However, instead of a gap being left in the crown, the stone that Mugwump had called The Misfit already filled the space. Koh-i-Noor levitated then came through the glass of the cabinet as if it were a non- entity, leaving no trace of its passage. As it left the cabinet a magnificent, multicoloured burst of light was thrown randomly into the room, cascading in all directions like a wonderful firework display. Rainbows, thought Olivia - rainbows spilled down the walls and across the ceiling, it was as if the stone was celebrating its new found freedom. Olivia was awe-struck, filled with emotions that brought tears to her eyes; Koh-i-Noor had been released and would be reunited with the body that was dying for her return.

# CHAPTER 8
# Mugwump and the
# Mercator's Projection

As they travelled the celestial sphere, Morgar patiently explained to Olivia how the constellations were mapped out in grid- like segments. Within the constellations were asterisms or star formations like the Big Dipper, Medusa's Head, and The Fish Hook. Olivia found the whole concept of space awe inspiring and settled down to enjoy the journey, travelling through time and space in a capsule created from the light force that the fairies themselves produced. The centre of the galaxy was a bright glow billowing out from an orange backdrop that sparkled with diamond-like stars. They travelled through the constellations of Pavo the peacock, Carina the ship's keel and Circinus the pair of compasses in the southern hemisphere and then Cetus the sea monster or whale and Delphinus the dolphin in the northern hemisphere. The journey, however, would take a different route from their last expedition to the birth place of rainbows. This time they would not cross the dangerous savannah that was home to the fearsome army ants that they had encountered last time, choosing now to approach their destination by water.

Mugwump held a nautical map, the Mercator's Projection, which would hopefully guide them firstly by sea, then upriver to their goal. The spectacle of the galaxy was sadly short- lived, for their journey through space was at light speed. Soon they found themselves on a deserted atoll surrounding a crystal clear lagoon. The atoll was small, uninhabited by humans and quite eerie. The silence was inexplicable, for the water that licked at the pink coral suggested noise but there was none, for in fact the water did not lap the shore as one would expect, but simply slid in and out in an unfathomable motion for there were no waves, the sea was in fact flat. Small trees, unlike any that Olivia had ever seen before, gathered in small clusters around the shore line. Their position, next to the water, seemed inappropriate, for their twisting roots seemed to recoil from the constant attention from the sea. Large buds pointed skyward from each twig and hummingbirds hovered, dipping their beaks into each pot-like flower in search of nectar. The number of birds looked too many to inhabit such a small atoll but Freya explained that the birds had all the food and water that they needed. Olivia soon noticed cone- shaped nests hanging from several branches of the trees and a small waterfall that seemed to originate from nowhere then disappear beneath the sand. Geography lessons had never taught Olivia of the existence of such a place and she wondered if it was known to the outside world.

Olivia's gaze had been so captivated by the view in front of her as she stepped from the light capsule, that she had not noticed the vista behind her. An archipelago or group of small islands seemed to float across the water like flotsam and jetsam far into the distance, their inhabitants, if any, invisible to the human eye.

"Morgar, are the islands inhabited?" asked Olivia.

"Olivia, these islands are unknown to the human race. They are home to all the creatures that have become extinct due to the carelessness of man. This does not reflect on you, Olivia, for we know that you are a kind and diligent human being who would not knowingly do harm to a creature, but there are people who show no respect for nature. We fairies have been entrusted with the husbandry of these unfortunate creatures. They now live under our protection and for the foreseeable future we have no intention of re-introducing them to your world, but you can rest assured that no creature has become truly extinct."

Olivia was speechless, her eyes downcast, for she was ashamed of the indifference shown to living creatures by her own race. She studied the endless islands, each home to one or more species of animal that the human race had been responsible for annihilating. Her mood became sombre and suddenly she was homesick. The shame she felt seemed to have built a barrier between herself and the fairies and she went to sit alone to reflect upon the wrong- doings of the world in which she lived.

It was Brokk who came to her side and sat at her feet. Looking up into her doleful eyes, he sympathised with her lack of understanding of all things that captured the essence of being a fairy. How fairies thought, what their morals were, what they had in common with the human race and how they perceived their world. All these things were a mystery to Olivia and Brokk seemed lost for words of consolation.

"Olivia, you should be very proud of yourself." Brokk began. Her eyes remained downcast.

"You are one of very few humans that have come to know us. You have proven yourself time and time again, I'm sure we will find some way to repay you."

Olivia's eyes remained focused on her feet that were shifting sand this way and that, without objective. Brokk paused, trying to think how to raise Olivia's spirits.

"Olivia, take my hand, I will show you the islands."

Olivia reluctantly took Brokk's hand and they glided up into the clear air. The water below looked like a giant warm bath, the lack of waves creating an aquamarine backdrop to the verdant archipelago.

"Look there, Olivia, do you see the dodos down there?"

Olivia saw several large birds, maybe a metre tall, slowly pecking away at fallen fruit. Their beaks were large and looked heavy, their movements slow and clumsy, they were unable to fly. Brokk explained that, related to pigeons and doves, they had lived on the island of Mauritius and had become extinct late in the 17th century. They now shared their sanctuary with great auks, another flightless bird related to penguins, which stood 30-34 inches tall and weighed around 5kg. Their glossy black and white feathers gleamed under the warm sun that had created a temperate climate for all the creatures under the protection of the fairies. Something then caught Olivia's attention, swimming in the sea around one of the small islands, a large seal-like creature gliding lazily amongst the seaweed. It had stout forelimbs and a whale-like tail. The head was small in proportion to its body and its skin looked thick, dark and resembled the bark of an old oak.

"It's a steller's sea cow, Olivia. They are perfectly tame - would you like to swim alongside one?"

Olivia declined, until another shape caught her eye. Swimming closely alongside the sea cow was a tiny figure that seemed similar in shape but was athletic in build and behaviour. At first Olivia thought that the tiny figure was trailing billowing seaweed, but looking more closely, she saw that it was hair. Soon the figure was joined by several more of its own kind and Olivia watched as they dived and tumbled around the sea cow that lazily went about its business. Olivia watched with fascination, for she could not think what these tiny creatures were. They plucked seaweed and fed it to the sea cow: they patted her and clung to her side as they glided along with her through the crystal clear water.

Rocks protruded from the water creating a landing place for the small creatures. They glided up the smooth rock surface and sunned themselves for a while. It wasn't until one of them turned over that Olivia could see exactly what they were – mermaids. Olivia gasped, causing Brokk to pause mid-air wondering what had caused Olivia to catch her breath so.

"Mermaids!" Olivia could not believe her eyes for she had thought that mermaids were mythical creatures. She watched, mesmerised, as the mermaids sunned themselves and groomed their hair: long cascading, wavy hair that was blond but had a hint of green to it. Their hair glistened in the sunlight, sparkling with a life of its own, covering the mermaids down to their waists. Below their waists Olivia could see their scaly lower bodies, thick muscular flesh culminating in an elegant fanned-out tail. The scales were large and shiny, reflecting a rainbow of colours that shimmered under the warm sunshine.

Suddenly Brokk dived, pulling Olivia with him, through the

warm air until they were close enough to speak to the mermaids. Brokk did not land on the rocks but hovered in front of the mermaids, giving Olivia a chance to study them more closely. Their eyes were dark blue, large and a little watery. They studied Olivia as intensely as she studied them. Their skin was perfect, blemish free, almost opaque with the quality of a beautiful pearl. Their facial features were somewhat fish-like in as far as their cheek bones were wide to accommodate their large eyes, and their mouths were surrounded by full lips. Their teeth, Brokk warned her, were razor sharp although they were not prone to bite.

There were three female mermaids and two males. The females communicated with one another as they watched Olivia, who got the distinct impression that they were laughing at her.

"Olivia, they are talking about your dark hair, they have only ever known blond hair. They want to touch you; do you want to land next to them?"

Olivia was only a little nervous as she agreed to land next to the mermaids, but the instant that she was on the rock with them, she relaxed. Their language was unknown to Olivia, their voices high pitched and fluid but Brokk seemed to understand them and laughed at their excitement. The females ran their fingers through Olivia's hair and tugged at her clothes. Their hands grabbed at Olivia's hands, a feeling that Olivia found slightly unpleasant for they were cold and damp as if they had just stepped out of a cold bath. Their movements out of water were somewhat ungainly, reminding Olivia of seals humping across beaches, but as the males slid back into the water she saw just how accomplished they were in their own environment. The speed at which they swam was incredible, their bodies twisting and turning with a fluid agility that overwhelmed her. One of the males swam at great speed back towards the rock then leaped out of the water, twisting and somersaulting in front of Olivia who screamed and clapped with excitement.

The scream sent the mermaids fleeing back into the water

and they were at once invisible. Pod leaped from Olivia's pocket to reprimand her.

"Do you think it wise to scream so, Olivia? Look what you have done- frightened everything in sight, for they are not used to humans with their overly zealous emotions!"

"Your voice is at a pitch that vibrates in their ears and frightens them," explained Brokk who sympathised with Olivia, whose face had flushed with an expression of regret that was most unbecoming.

"Go into the water, Olivia, they will come back to see you," encouraged Brokk.

"Olivia, Brokk," called Morgar. "We are ready to set sail: The Koh-i-Noor diamond becomes impatient."

Olivia's disappointment was tragically written all over her face for she longed to swim with the mermaids, however the reason for their mission was now all- important. They must re-unite the heart of Koh-i-Noor with the body. That is what their journey was about, so reluctantly Olivia took Brokk's hand. They flew upwards towards the frolic of fairies, passing lush islands home to a mishmash of unidentifiable creatures, large and small.

"Brokk, look down there on that island, do you see? A beautiful white stallion grazing, look Brokk, enormous butterflies and strange insects are flying around him." Olivia pondered on the fact that horses were certainly not extinct as she watched the shimmering white hind quarters of the horse, whose head was held low, munching on the tall sweet grass. Brokk took no notice as he flew towards the frolic. Suddenly the horse lifted his head high, ears alert. He swished his dappled grey tail as his mouth munched on the trailing grasses. His stance was proud and fearless his eyes bright and watchful.

"Brokk," shouted Olivia, but Brokk paid little heed to Olivia's voice as it trailed off into astonished silence.

"Brokk – it's a unicorn."

# CHAPTER 9
# Skidbladnir

Olivia looked back at the small islands with a heavy heart. She wondered if, in her lifetime, it would ever be possible to return and enjoy the wonders of this mystical place. The reed craft, in which they now sailed up a wide, fast flowing river, was up-turned to a point at each end reminding Olivia of a genie's shoe. Olivia assumed the fairies had built the boat whilst Brokk and she were exploring the islands; it was made of thick woven reeds and had a linen awning to enable them to shelter from the scorching sun. The river was bumpy, carrying them rapidly up-stream with help from a small triangular sail. The Koh-i-Noor diamond sat proudly in the centre of the small craft: its translucent colours becoming stronger and brighter with each lap of their voyage.

Clouds, unusual in their formation, scudded across the sky above their heads as if they were enticing the craft forward in an attempt to hasten the journey. The small triangular sail billowed as the wind, Bora, blew into it with a robust enthusiasm that seemed to run through the frolic of fairies that began to fidget and chant in a behavioural pattern that Olivia had witnessed before. From the banks of the river animals began to screech and scream - Olivia could see trees and bushes moving violently with the passage of the unknown creatures that traced their progress.

Freya sat beside Olivia and once her chanting stopped she told Olivia that their craft was called Skidbladnir. It could not only sail on the water but also through the air. There were more sails to be hoisted if necessary but that would take them skyward and Mugwump wanted to approach the savannah by water. The boat had not in fact been built in her absence as Olivia thought, but had been carried all this way by Morgar, as it was possible to fold the boat down and pack it into the pouch that he carried at his waist, thus it was easy to assemble. This was a concept that Olivia could not understand, considering the size and weight of the craft so she put it down to magic. As she watched the shoreline whizz by, she wondered just how much of what the fairies did involved magic, for to be truthful she had witnessed very few mystical events and wondered if for some reason the fairies did not want her to understand their true paranormal potential. She felt that perhaps they preferred her to see their weaknesses and remain oblivious to their powers.

"My friends," said Mugwump. "We have come this far safely and without loss. The next leg of our journey should deliver us at last to our destination -the crevasse on the savannah that holds the body of Koh-i-Noor. We have her heart safely here with us and we will not let her down. We will re-unite her body with her heart and our beloved rainbows will bedazzle us once more. We have only to get upstream and through a small expanse of rain forest to reach our goal. May our journey be blessed by the luck of Bardzack and our success written in The Leaves of Gerfalcon - now let us drink our malmsey wine and prepare ourselves for whatever lies ahead."

The mood amongst the fairies became festive and upbeat. Olivia joined them in a toast to Bardzack, enjoying the malmsey wine with its sweet heady bouquet. The boat, Skidbladnir, seemed to sail itself, rising over the rough water, giving the crew a smooth ride as they drank their wine, laughing and telling Olivia stories from earlier adventures. The noise from the jungle that enclosed the river on both sides seemed to be lost as the crew enjoyed a time of camaraderie and frivolity.

The day had been both long and arduous so Olivia let the voices of the frolic pass over her head as she sat quietly with her own thoughts. The wine had calmed her, relaxing both body and mind as their journey continued. Without warning, however, in the blink of an eye, the waters changed from the tranquil steady flow that they had all been enjoying to a noisy rushing torrent. The boat leaped and dropped with a ferocity that scared Olivia, whose back and neck jarred with each fall of the boat. Olivia grabbed for Freya but alas not on time for Olivia was thrown from the boat, as were the fairies and the Koh-i-Noor diamond. But instead of finding herself in the water gasping for air as she had expected, she found that Skidbladnir, the boat, had split into six separate smaller boats transporting her and the fairies separately.

Each canoe- shaped vessel had a large paddle with a handle at one end but only Olivia's canoe held the Koh-i-Noor diamond. Olivia looked over to the fairies in the other five canoes - each had taken up their paddle and started to use it with great expertise. Olivia did likewise, holding one hand on the shaft of the paddle, the other grasping the handle. With each pull of the paddle, beads of perspiration began to glisten on her forehead. The water had taken on a fiery anger that threw the fairies this way and that. The torrent up ahead was creating giant white horses that leaped and fell, causing great waves to impede their progress. Olivia screamed as her canoe was lifted high above the river giving her a clear view of the impending drop down the thunderous waterfall just ahead of her.

The fall, that Olivia had thought would throw her from the canoe and possibly kill her, was unimaginably peaceful. The canoe went into a slow motion free fall that kept Olivia comfortably upright in her seat, the Koh-i-Noor diamond resting safely beside her. There was a small thud at the bottom, although the soft reeds took the impact as she rejoined the becalmed river, giving her time to gather her thoughts. Looking around she could not see the fairies, however, she was confident that they would be following her down the waterfall as there was no possible way for them to avoid it.

She decided to paddle to the edge of the river where she could wait for them but the water, or was it the paddle, now had a mind of its own. However hard she pulled the paddle through the water to take her in one direction, the current did not respond to her effort. The small craft started to move slowly away from the bank and back into the central flow of the river.

Olivia, realising the futility of her endeavour, sat anxiously at the mercy of her canoe, clasping the soft reeds with white knuckles. She looked down, noticing for the first time that her Sheath of Coeval lay at her feet. Although this gave her comfort, she could not think how this would help her in this instance. The Koh-i-Noor diamond sparkled with anticipation, throwing out bright lights to dance across Olivia's crest-fallen face– but she did not share its optimism.

The canoe, skimming happily across the water, obviously had a destination in mind. This became apparent as it led Olivia through a curtain of chilling water which fell from a smaller waterfall, and into sudden darkness. Olivia's hair clung damply to her face but that was the least of her worries. She found herself in a dark, underground labyrinth, the coldness reaching out and touching her as disturbingly as did her tangled wet hair. The canoe continued on its predestined course to who knew where or for what purpose. Was someone or something after the diamond?

The water swirled, making Olivia's stomach queasy, taking the small canoe on a roller coaster ride into the depth of the labyrinth. The darkness that surrounded Olivia was almost tangible and her fear grew with astonishing rapidity. She cowered low in the boat in a vain attempt to protect herself but the darkness touched her body and soul until she let out a shrill scream. Her voice echoed and reverberated off the jagged walls and ceilings, rolling down invisible corridors that led into even darker places. A chill wafted past Olivia's ears, an ill wind that taunted her with its mischievous fingers, tickling and whispering, sending goose bumps down her spine. Olivia covered her ears and screwed herself up into a tight ball on the floor of the canoe.

Olivia's courage had totally deserted her and she wished that she had never got to know the fairies. It was at that moment that she felt the Sheath of Coeval under her knees. A glimmer of hope shone through the darkness as she lifted the sheath high, remembering what she had been told. "The sheath can act as a beacon should you get separated from us." Olivia grabbed the sheath with both hands, lifting it high as she brought herself to a kneeling position. At once the bright light force from the sheath illuminated the cavernous labyrinth. Her worst fears played out in front of her as she watched numerous lizards and crustaceans crawl and slither in a nightmarish fashion across the walls, then plop into the water to flee from the light.

Olivia found it impossible to control the shaking of her hands which caused the light force to dance a jittery tango across a volcanic backdrop. However, now that Olivia had light, her courage seemed to renew itself. She tried to think rationally but she had to admit to herself that she was totally lost. Then to her horror, a noise bounced off the walls, coming from one of the dark corridors. The noise was not in itself frightening, only in as far as something unknown to Olivia shared her dungeon-like cavern. The pitch and tone seemed strangely familiar, which gave Olivia some small shred of comfort but, when the water erupted and two small hands grabbed the side of the canoe, Olivia nearly expired.

A beautiful face with large blue eyes peered into the canoe, an elegant fanned- out tail keeping the mermaid afloat next to the boat. The mermaid seemed only interested in the Koh-i-Noor diamond that was thankfully still safe within the canoe. The mermaid's eyes then caught Olivia's eyes - the large aquamarine orbs were full of compassion that filled Olivia with a sense of security in the midst of this unrelenting torment. The little mermaid reached into the canoe and touched the Koh-i-Noor diamond, at which point it seemed to come to life. Lights shone into the darkness, multicoloured lights that sparkled across the water. A rainbow, Olivia thought, it is showing me the right path to take. The mermaid began to sing - her hair streaming out behind her as she gently slid from the side of the canoe back into the black water and started to swim in the direction of the lights. The rainbow that twinkled across the water took the canoe down one of the large corridors that led off from the cavern in which Olivia had found herself.

The mermaid's singing was haunting, unearthly, a soft deep contralto that echoed down alleyways. No words were audible but Olivia found the rhythm so intoxicating that she temporarily forgot where she was - lost in the moment. She felt an all-consuming sense of relief, for the loneliness that she had experienced in the darkness had been unbearable. With a suddenness that surprised her, Olivia's mood lifted as she watched the mermaid's gentle passage in front of the canoe. The tail moved slowly up and down, giving Olivia a chance to study the beautiful creature, her scales as vividly coloured as the glistening rainbow that spread across the water before her. Her voice was the impetus that pulled the canoe forward for, each time her voice rose, the little boat hurried forward.

Soon daylight could be seen as a far off glint penetrating the darkness. The canoe raced forward, overtaking the mermaid who once again caught hold of the boat, pulling herself upwards. She looked into Olivia's eyes, her voice intent on communicating with Olivia, who sadly could not interpret a word. The mermaid reached out and took Olivia's hand - she spoke purposefully and turned Olivia's hand palm up. She traced the lines on the palm of Olivia's hand, and then placed a glistening object into it. A pearl - a large orb that gleamed into the darkness- but before Olivia could respond the mermaid was gone.

Olivia felt a painful sense of loss as she heard the splash of the mermaid's tail, slowly withdrawing from the corridor down which Olivia now sped. The dot of light at the end of the corridor grew brighter and larger with every inch of her progress until Olivia burst out into daylight on a jet stream of warm air. The little sail filled with the warm wind, lifting the canoe into the air and taking it high above a green canopy that shaded a lush rain forest. Was it the forest that led to the crevasse on the savannah, wondered Olivia.

Thankful that she could now breathe clean warm air, Olivia took a moment to look at the pearl. It was not plain but had inscriptions carved into it and a weight that seemed unnatural for its size. Head held low, studying her gift, Olivia failed to notice the descent of the boat in which she sailed so perilously through the air. The thud onto land jolted Olivia from her thoughts as the boat came to a standstill. Looking up she squealed with delight for there before her were Brokk, Mugwump and Morgar. Freya and Enya were sheltering under a large fern-like plant that dripped with the humidity of the forest. They did not look pleased but Olivia leaped from the boat and ran to give Morgar a hug.

"Do you think it wise to hold Morgar so tightly? You may crease his wings," reprimanded Pod, who had sprung from Olivia's pocket. However Olivia was too pleased at seeing her companions to take any notice of Pod. The reunion was sadly short lived for the urgency to reunite the heart and the body of Koh-i-Noor was now all too demanding. Mugwump retrieved the diamond from the canoe and the six set off once more in relatively high spirits, although Olivia could tell that Mugwump had not been pleased with her temporary disappearance. The pearl that had been given to her was now held closely in her pocket with Pod to guard it, and for the moment forgotten.

The path through the rain forest led directly out onto the savannah, the crevasse a dark split on the horizon. The glow from the heart of the Koh-i-Noor diamond increased with every step taken, however, Olivia and the fairies could not help but notice that the closer they got to the crevasse the more arid the terrain became. The ground seemed infertile, dust billowing up with each foot- fall, causing Olivia to cough and the fairies to cover their mouths with their wings. Dusty dry beetles walked solemnly by, their eyes unseeing, their direction without purpose. Were the fairies too late, had the body of Koh-i-Noor given in to grief?

They reached the crevasse at nightfall, the natural light moderately enhanced by a few dull stars. The mood amongst the fairies was grave, each thinking the worst but not voicing it. Mugwump held the heart of Koh-i-Noor up but the brilliance did not outshine the lacklustre stars that hung in the sky above their heads. In fact the light seemed to drain from its core in front of their eyes. The six tired warriors sat in a circle, the diamond in their midst. The chanting started at midnight and lasted until dawn. There was no celebratory dawn chorus that day, just a greyness that seemed to cover both land and sky. No malmsey wine was drunk to lift their mood, no mammal, bird or insect moved.

Tears rolled down Olivia's cheeks as Mugwump stood, once again holding the heart of Koh-i-Noor up high. He moved to the edge of the crevasse, peering deep into the gloom. The outline of the body of Koh-i-Noor could be seen, jagged, lifeless and opaque. Overhead a large bird circled, reminding Olivia of a vulture waiting for death. As it came closer however, she noticed that the bird was not bare-headed and ugly, but actually colourful and elegant causing Olivia to sense that she was female. As she circled, her voice sailed out across the savannah, a voice that Olivia found vaguely familiar. Somehow the timbre of the notes reminded her of the mermaid, the sequence of the syllables unmistakeable. Olivia took the pearl from her pocket and studied the inscriptions more closely.

"Unbelievable!" Olivia shrieked, startling the fairies and making Pod leap from his pocket. "Look, Pod – the inscription!"

Olivia leaped to her feet and ran to Mugwump, snatching the diamond from his hand. The fairies stood in wonderment as Olivia held the gem up high to the circling bird that was rapidly descending. The yellow talon- like feet snatched the gem from Olivia's upheld hand, the gust of wind from the bird's wings nearly knocking Olivia into the crevasse. The bird circled upwards once more then plummeted into the gaping crevasse like a ravenous sea bird diving for fish, her wings held closely to her body. In that moment Olivia knew that the bird would not survive and her elation turned to sorrow. The poignant voice of the mermaid was in fact the bird's swan song.

There was no noise from the crevasse as the frolic waited for some reaction. The bird, as Olivia had predicted, did not resurface - a funereal silence hung in the air. Time stood still, dark clouds rumbled overhead and the temperature dropped suddenly. A bolt of lightning was thrown from the darkest of clouds, hitting the centre of the crevasse, causing sparks to fly into the air like fireworks. Then it started, like a volcanic eruption spitting out molten rock, sparks of pure white light billowed upwards spreading in all directions. Bright lights, thought Olivia, lights that were a prelude to the multicoloured beams that exploded from the depths of the crevasse to dance in and out of the asteroids, rushing across the sky that had become an inconsequential backdrop for the spectacle. Rainbows, hundreds of them, frolicked in the atmosphere searching out new trails, their re-birth a joy for the world to see. Koh-i-Noor was whole again.

The frolic knew their work was done. Was it safe to return home that night across skies that were alive with a mystical display of colours? In their light capsule they followed their trajectory. All was calm - all was bright, thought Olivia. She clasped the pearl deep in her pocket, feeling the weight and wondering what it might hold within. In bed that night, after her father, who had been disturbed from his slumber, had tucked her in and kissed her goodnight, Olivia lay tracing the lines carved deeply into the pearl with her finger. Soon, however, her sleepy lids drooped, exhaustion overwhelmed her, swallowing her up into a dream- free sleep that rendered her incapable of deciphering the rest of the inscription, or of seeing the pearl's contents as, like a chrysalis splitting open to reveal a butterfly, the hard outer shell cracked, displaying what lay at its heart.

"Olivia," screamed Pod, "do you think it wise to sleep at a time like this?" But Olivia could not be woken.